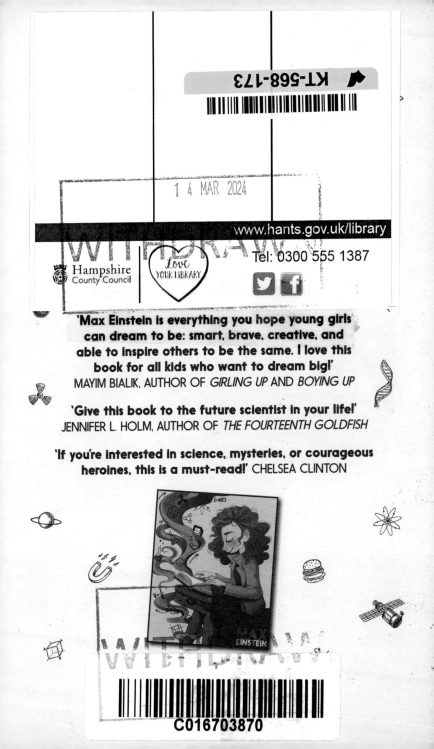

'Max Einstein is everything you hope young girls can dream to be: smart, brave, creative, and able to inspire others to be the same. I love this book for all kids who want to dream big!'
MAYIM BIALIK, AUTHOR OF *GIRLING UP* AND *BOYING UP*

'Give this book to the future scientist in your life!'
JENNIFER L. HOLM, AUTHOR OF *THE FOURTEENTH GOLDFISH*

'If you're interested in science, mysteries, or courageous heroines, this is a must-read!' CHELSEA CLINTON

MAX EINSTEIN

MAX EINSTEIN

AGE: Twelve

HAIR: Crazy, curly and red!

HOMETOWN: New York City

FAVORITE SUBJECT: Science

FAVORITE GAME: Chess

FAVORITE FOOD: Chinese

FAVORITE CELEBRITY: Albert Einstein — duh!

$V = \dfrac{I}{R}$

MAX EINSTEIN

THE GENIUS EXPERIMENT

JAMES PATTERSON
AND CHRIS GRABENSTEIN

Illustrated by Beverly Johnson

1 3 5 7 9 10 8 6 4 2

Young Arrow
20 Vauxhall Bridge Road
London SW1V 2SA

Young Arrow is part of the Penguin Random House group of companies
whose addresses can be found at global.penguinrandomhouse.com

Penguin
Random House
UK

First published by Young Arrow in 2018
This edition published in paperback by Young Arrow in 2019

www.penguin.co.uk

A CIP catalogue record for this book is available from the British Library

ISBN 9781784759827

Printed and bound in Great Britain by Clays Ltd, Elcograf S.p.A.

Penguin Random House is committed to a sustainable future for our
business, our readers and our planet. This book is made from Forest
Stewardship Council® certified paper.

To the children who will inherit this earth
and make it a far better place than we did.
—JP and CG

MAX EINSTEIN
EINSTEIN
THE GENIUS EXPERIMENT

Imagination is more
important than knowledge.

- Albert Einstein

1

The stench of horse manure woke Max Einstein with a jolt.

"Of course!"

Even though she was shivering, she threw off her blanket and hopped out of bed. Actually, it wasn't really a bed. More like a lumpy, water-stained mattress with frayed seams. But that didn't matter. Ideas could come wherever they wanted.

She raced down the dark hall. The floorboards—bare planks laid across rough beams—creaked and wobbled with every step. Her red hair, of course, was a bouncing tangle of wild curls. It was always a bouncing tangle of wild curls.

Max rapped her knuckles on a lopsided door hanging off rusty hinges.

1

"Mr. Kennedy?" She knocked again. "Mr. Kennedy?"

"What the…" came a sleepy mumble. "Max? Are you okay?"

Max took that question as permission to enter Mr. Kennedy's apartment. She practically burst through his wonky door.

"I'm fine, Mr. Kennedy. In fact, I'm better than fine! I've got something great here! At least I think it's something great. Anyway, it's really, really cool. This idea could change everything. It could save our world. It's what Mr. Albert Einstein would've called an 'aha' moment."

"Maxine?"

"Yes, Mr. Kennedy?"

"It's six o'clock in the morning, girl."

"Is it? Sorry about the inconvenient hour. But you never know when a brainstorm will strike, do you?"

"No. Not with *you*, anyway…"

Max was wearing a floppy trench coat over her shabby sweater. Lately, she'd been sleeping in the sweater under a scratchy horse blanket because her so-called bedroom was, just like Mr. Kennedy's, extremely cold.

The tall and sturdy black man, his hair flecked with patches of white, creaked out of bed and rubbed some of the sleep out of his eyes. He slid his bare feet into shoes he had fashioned out of cardboard and old newspapers.

2

"Hang on," he said. "Need to put on my bedroom slippers here…"

"Because the floor's so cold," said Max.

"Huh?"

"You needed to improvise those bedroom slippers because the floor's cold every morning. Correct?"

"Maxine—we're sleeping, uninvited, above a horse stable. Of course the floors are cold. And, in case you haven't noticed, the place doesn't smell so good, either."

Max, Mr. Kennedy, and about a half-dozen other homeless people were what New York City called "squatters." That meant they were living rent-free in the vacant floors above a horse stable. The first two floors of the building housed a parking garage for Central Park carriages and stalls for the horses that pulled them. The top three floors? As far as the owner of the building knew, they were vacant.

"Winter is coming, Mr. Kennedy. We have no central heating system."

"Nope. We sure don't. You know why? Because we don't pay rent, Max!"

"Be that as it may, in the coming weeks, these floors will only become colder. Soon, we could all freeze to death. Even if we were to board up all the windows—"

"That's not gonna happen," said Mr. Kennedy. "We

3

need the ventilation. All that horse manure downstairs, stinking up the place…"

"Exactly! That's precisely what I wanted to talk to you about. That's my big idea. *Horse manure!*"

2

"It's simple, really, Mr. Kennedy," said Max, moving to the cracked plaster wall and finding a patch that wasn't covered with graffiti.

She pulled a thick stub of chalk out her baggy sweater pocket and started sketching on the wall, turning it into her blackboard.

"Please hear me out, sir. Try to see what I see."

Max, who enjoyed drawing in a beat-up sketchbook she rescued from a Dumpster, chalked in a lump of circles radiating stink marks. She labeled it "manure/biofuel."

"To stay warm this winter, all we have to do is arrange a meeting with Mr. Sammy Monk."

"The owner of this building?" said Mr. Kennedy,

skeptically. "The landlord who doesn't even know we're here? *That* Mr. Sammy Monk?"

"Yes, sir," said Max, totally engrossed in the diagram she was drafting on the wall. "We need to convince him to let us have all of his horse manure."

Mr. Kennedy stood up. "All of his manure? Now why on earth would we want that, Max? It's manure!"

"Well, once we have access to the manure, I will design and engineer a green gas mill for the upstairs apartments."

"A green what mill?"

"Gas, sir. We can rig up an anaerobic digester that will turn the horse manure into biogas, which we can then combust to generate electricity and heat."

"You want to burn horse manure gas?"

"Exactly! Anaerobic digestion is a series of biological processes in which microorganisms break down biodegradable material, such as horse manure, in the absence of oxygen, which is what 'anaerobic' means. That's the solution to our heating and power problems."

"You sure you're just twelve years old?"

"Yes. As far as I know."

Mr. Kennedy gave Max a look that she, unfortunately, was used to seeing. The look said she was crazy. Nuts. Off her rocker. But Max never let "the look" upset her. It was like Albert Einstein said, "Great spirits have always

6

encountered violent opposition from mediocre minds."

Not that Mr. Kennedy had a mediocre mind. Max just wasn't doing a good enough job explaining her bold new breakthrough idea. Sometimes, the ideas came into her head so fast they came out of her mouth in a mumbled jumble.

"All we need, Mr. Kennedy, is an airtight container—something between the size of an oil drum and a tanker truck." She sketched a boxy cube fenced in by a pen of steel posts. "Heavy plastic would be best, of course. And it would be good if it had a cage of galvanized iron bars surrounding it. Then we just have to measure and cut three different pipes—one for feeding in the manure, one for the gas outlet, and one for displaced liquid fertilizer. We would insert these conduits into the tank through a universal seal, hook up the appropriate plumbing, and we'd be good to go."

Mr. Kennedy stroked his stubbly chin and admired Max's detailed design of the device sketched on the flaking wall.

"A brilliant idea, Max," he said. "Like always."

Max allowed herself a small, proud smile.

"Thank you, Mr. Kennedy."

"Slight problem."

"What's that, sir?"

"Well, that container there. The cube. That's what? Ten feet by ten feet by ten feet?"

"About."

"And you say you need a cage of bars around it. You also mentioned three pipes. And plumbing. Then I figure you're going to need a furnace to burn the horse manure gas, turn it into heat."

Max nodded. "And a generator. To spin our own electricity."

"Right. Won't that cost a whole lot of money?"

Max lowered her chalk. "I suppose so."

"And have you ever noticed the one thing most people squatting in this building don't have?"

Max pursed her lips. "Money?"

"Uhm-hmm. Exactly."

Max tucked the stubby chalk back into her sweater pocket and dusted off her pale, cold hands.

"Point taken, Mr. Kennedy. As usual, I need to be more practical. I'll get back to you with a better plan. I'll get back to you before winter comes."

"Great. But, Max?"

"Yes, sir?"

Mr. Kennedy climbed back into his lumpy bed and pulled up the blanket.

"Just don't get back to me before seven o'clock, okay?"

3

Max glanced at her watch.

It was only 6:17 a.m. She, unlike Mr. Kennedy, was an early riser. Always had been, probably always would be. The morning, especially that quiet space between dreaming and total wakefulness, was when most of her massive ideas floated through her drowsy brain. The ideas helped tamp down the sadness that could come in those same quiet times. A sadness that all orphans probably shared. Made more intense because Max had no idea who either of her parents were.

Max creaked her way back up the hall to her room as quietly as she could. She could hear Mr. Kennedy already snoring behind her.

Max had decorated her own sleeping space in the stables

building the same way she had decorated all the rooms she had ever temporarily lived in: by propping open her battered old suitcase on its side to turn it into a display case for all things Albert Einstein. Books by and about the famous scientist were lined along the bottom like a bookshelf. Both lids were filled with her collection of Einstein photographs and quotes. She even had an Einstein bobblehead doll she'd found, once upon a time, in a museum store dumpster. She used it as a bookend.

Max couldn't remember where the suitcase came from. She'd just always had it. It was older than her rumpled knit sweater, and that thing was an antique.

The oldest photograph in her collection, the one that someone other than Max (she didn't know who) had pasted inside the suitcase lid so long ago that its edges were curling, showed the great professor lost in thought. He had a bushy mustache and long, unkempt hair. His hands were clasped together, almost as if in prayer. His eyes were gazing up toward infinity.

That photograph was Max's oldest memory. And since she never knew her own parents, at an early age, Max found herself talking to the kind, grandfatherly man at bedtime. He was a very good listener. She became curious as to who the mystery man might be, and that's how her lifelong infatuation with all things Einstein began.

11

Like how he was born in Germany but had to leave his home before the Second World War. And how he was so busy thinking of big, amazing ideas, he sometimes forgot to pay attention to his job at the patent office. They had a lot in common.

Next to the photograph was Max's absolute favorite Einstein quote: "Imagination is more important than knowledge."

"Unless, of course, you don't have the money to make the things you dream up come true," Max muttered.

Mr. Kennedy was right.

She couldn't afford to build her green gas mill. And she couldn't ask Mr. Sammy Monk for his horse manure or anything else because Mr. Sammy Monk couldn't know anybody was living in the abandoned floors of his horse stable. She'd just have to imagine a different solution to the squatters' heating dilemma. One that didn't cost a dime and could be created out of someone else's discarded scraps.

Max turned to her computer, which she had built herself from found parts. It was amazing what some people in New York City tossed to the curb on garbage pickup days. Max had been able to solder together (with a perfectly good soldering iron someone had thrown out) enough discarded circuit boards, unwanted wiring, abandoned processors, rejected keyboards, and one slightly blemished retina screen from a cast-off MacBook Pro to create a machine that whirred even faster than her mind.

She also had free wi-fi, thanks to the Link NYC public hot spot system. She could even recharge her computer's batteries (discovered abandoned behind one of the city's glossy Apple stores) at the kiosk just down the block from the stables. (Reliable wi-fi was one of the main reasons Max had selected her current accommodations. Easy access to a top-flight school was the other.)

Max clicked open a browser and went back to the internet page she had bookmarked the night before.

It was a nightmarish news report about children as young as seven "working in perilous conditions in the Democratic Republic of the Congo to mine cobalt that ends up in smartphones, cars, and computers sold to millions across the world." The children, as many as forty thousand, were being paid one dollar a day to do backbreaking work. They were also helping make a shadowy international business consortium called the Corp very, very, *very* rich.

The story broke Max's heart.

Because Max's heart, like her hero Dr. Einstein's, was huge.

4

Max was packing her bookbag for school when she heard a commotion down on the street.

She dropped her backpack and raced to the nearest dirt-smeared window to peer through a hole in the glass.

She saw two police cars. Their roof bar lights were swirling. Even from four stories up, Max could hear snatches of orders crackling out of the cruiser's dashboard radio: "Squatters…eviction…arrest…trespassing…"

Then she saw two officers, a man and a woman, escorting Mrs. Rabinowitz—a sweet widow who lived on the third floor—out of the building and toward their police car. Mrs. Rabinowitz's frumpy housecoat was flapping in the breeze, exposing her knee-high stockings.

15

"There're more squatters upstairs," said the female cop. "We may need backup."

"On it," said a cop, casually leaning up against one of the cruisers with a radio mic in his hand. He seemed to be the man in charge. "Yeah, this is Alpha Three Five Oh," he said matter-of-factly into his microphone. "One suspect in custody. More in building. Request backup."

Max had heard enough.

She raced down four flights of steep, switchback staircases and into the bright morning light.

"Excuse me, officers," she said, holding up a hand to shield her eyes from the sun. "Might I have a word?"

"What? Who are you, kid?" asked the cop who seemed to be in charge.

"Maxine Einstein, sir."

"Like the egghead Einstein? The E equals M-C squared guy?"

Max didn't answer. Instead, she tried to keep the conversation focused and on point. She had learned long ago that it was hard to achieve your desired scientific outcome if you let your mind wander into trivialities.

"Why are you arresting Mrs. Rabinowitz?" she asked, her voice strong and firm.

"Because, little Miss Einstein, your friend here is a squatter. She can't live in this building without paying rent.

Neither can any of those other people upstairs." The police officer gave Max a menacing look. "Neither can you, kid."

"Officer, if I may, are you familiar with the legal term 'adverse possession'?"

"Oh. So now you're a little lawyer?"

"No, officer. I have not completed the necessary course of study, nor have I passed the New York State bar exam. However, I do know that adverse possession is the legal term for occupying someone else's property. When you do so, you obtain what are known as 'squatter's rights.' In the state of New York, a person has to live on the property openly and without permission of the owner for a period of at least ten uninterrupted years to be able to claim adverse possession."

"You telling me these folks have been squatting over Mr. Monk's stables for more than ten years and he just now called us about it?"

"No. I believe the squatters have only been in possession of this particular premises for six or seven months. I will have to check with Mr. Kennedy for specifics."

"Well, little Miss Einstein, six or seven months isn't ten years."

"True. However, in New York *City* the laws are different than they are in New York *State*. We have our own set of adverse possession laws, which you, of course, are sworn to uphold. In New York City, sir, a person is granted squatter's rights after just thirty days."

The cop stared at Max with a blank expression on his face. She often had that effect on people.

"After thirty days," she continued, "a New York City squatter has the right to continue living in a building until the actual owner—in this case, Mr. Sammy Monk—goes through the lengthy and, I am told, very expensive process of legal eviction. From my understanding, that can take up to a year. Sometimes longer."

The other police officers were now staring at the one holding the radio microphone, wondering what to do next. Two of them still had their hands gripped on Mrs. Rabinowitz's arms, waiting for orders.

The officer in charge shook his head.

"Let her go."

The other officers did.

Mrs. Rabinowitz rubbed her arms where the police had been clutching them and hurried over to Max to give her a kiss.

"Thank you, dear," she whispered.

"You're welcome, Mrs. Rabinowitz. Glad I could be of assistance."

"I found a bagel with cream cheese yesterday. Want it?"

"No, thank you, Mrs. Rabinowitz. I already ate break-fast."

"Good. It's the most important meal of the day…"

The frail widow scurried back into the stables.

"Hey, Einstein?" said the lead cop.

"Yes, sir?"

"What school do you go to? I wanna send my son there."

5

Max ran upstairs to grab her backpack.

The discussion with the police officer had knocked her off her very rigid schedule.

She had to force herself to stay organized—not always easy when you're absentminded and prone to what Mr. Kennedy called "too much daydreaming." He thought you should only dream while you were asleep. "You know—nightdreaming!"

But Max didn't have a mother or father to tell her when it was time to wake up, go to bed, do her homework, eat her vegetables, turn off the TV, or hurry because she'd miss the subway if she didn't. Max was completely on her own.

Well, not completely. She had Mr. Kennedy, Mrs. Rabinowitz, and the other squatters in the building. But, to be

20

honest, none of them really possessed what Max would call "stellar time-management skills."

But they loved her and she loved them back. That was good enough for Max. The homeless people camping out above the stables were the closest thing she'd had to family in a long time. Max didn't even know if "Einstein" was her real family name. Was she related to the famous genius?

She didn't know.

Max Einstein had no idea who she was, where she came from, how she ended up in New York City, or where she got the name Max Einstein. She liked to think of it as the one great mystery in life that she couldn't begin to solve, especially not today. She was running late (even for her).

"Have a good day at school, Max!" Mrs. Rabinowitz cried out as Max bounded down the staircase to the third floor.

"Thank you!"

"You sure you don't want half of this bagel? It's got *strawberry* cream cheese."

"No, thanks. Gotta run."

She made it to the main floor of the stables. "Morning, Domino, Kit Kat, and Opie!" she cried.

The horses whinnied in their stalls and flicked their tails.

"Keep making manure, guys," said Max. "One day, we're going to build that green gas mill!"

The day after I win the lottery, she thought.

The horse stables were on the western edge of Manhattan, close to the Hudson River. Max had to dash four blocks east and a couple blocks south to take the downtown subway at West 50th Street and Eighth Avenue.

She caught a lucky break. A train screeched into the station just as she hurdled down the steps. Max leaped through the doors, which were closing like a hungry steel mouth, and tumbled into the crowded car.

"Sorry," she said, as she bumped into a clump of commuters clutching a pole. She found a handhold just before the train lurched forward. When it did, she fell slightly backward because of, well, physics. Sir Isaac Newton, the granddaddy of modern physics, developed laws of motion, including the one that says a body at rest tends to stay at rest—even when a train accelerated forward.

That's exactly what Max's body (and all the other bodies crammed into the rush hour train) did. When the train came to a stop, they would all lurch forward because, by then, their bodies would be in motion and tending to stay in motion.

While the subway car rocked south at thirty miles per hour, Max observed a fly zipping through the car, headed north.

So how fast is the fly flying? she wondered with a grin. *It's all relative, of course.*

That was one of Albert Einstein's most famous ideas: the theory of relativity.

How fast the fly was flying *uptown* on a subway car hurtling *downtown* depended on how you measured things. It was all *relative* to your perspective.

The fly was, simultaneously, going five miles per hour in one direction and twenty-five in the other.

Someone standing in the subway tunnel as the train rumbled past (a very dumb idea, especially for a scientist) would measure the fly's speed as moving *south* at twenty-five miles per hour.

But, inside the car, Max perceived it as moving five miles per hour *north*.

Until a big guy, two poles up, plucked the poor little bug out of the air in mid-flight and smooshed it.

Then it wasn't moving at all.

6

Nine minutes later, Max emerged from the West 4th Street station and glanced at her watch.

She was back on schedule. She saw some kids playing a frantic game of pickup basketball, their bookbags leaning up against the chain-link fence penning in the court. She wondered what that would be like. To play on the way to school. Max didn't spend much time with other children. There weren't very many in her world. In a weird way, Albert Einstein was probably her best friend.

As she walked along, she noticed all sorts of things that reminded her of Einstein's incredible contributions to the modern world—if only he were alive to see them.

She saw a tourist couple consulting a map app on their smartphone. The app, of course, relied on GPS to pinpoint their precise location on the island of Manhattan. It bounced a signal off satellites orbiting the Earth. The app could help them find the nearest Starbucks with GPS, which worked because of Einstein's theory of relativity and something he called *time dilation*. Smartphones were smart because Einstein was smarter.

Max glanced at her watch. She had time to stop by Washington Square Park and see if Mr. Weinstock was interested in a quick game of speed chess.

Mr. Leonard "Lenny" Weinstock claimed to be from London, England. Max was never certain if he was telling her the truth about that. Or the fact that he graduated from Oxford. Or that he met the queen. "On several different occasions, mind you."

Max just knew he was a nice old man with a very proper British accent who always wore checked shirts, a safari vest, and a flat cap—the kind cabbies used to wear. Mr. Weinstock also liked to play chess as much as Max did.

"Ah, good morning, Maxine," he said when Max plopped down on the bench opposite him at one of the park's many outdoor chess tables.

"Good morning, Mr. Weinstock."

"Care for a game?"

"Yes, sir. If you're up for it."

"Of course, dear. I believe you're currently ahead in our ongoing tally of pairings."

"Yes, sir. Slightly."

In truth, Max had won far more games against Mr. Weinstock than she had lost. And the ones she did lose, she lost on purpose. There really was no need to crush Mr. Weinstock's fighting spirit with a string of unrelenting defeats. As it was, he was just about the only regular in Washington Square Park who was willing to play against Max Einstein. Her reputation preceded her.

"Blitz, bullet, or lightning?" asked Mr. Weinstock, referring to the various levels of speed chess.

"Is lightning okay today?" asked Max. "I don't want to be late for school."

"Right you are. Lightning it is, then."

Mr. Weinstock bopped a button on top of a digital timer. Each player would have ten seconds to ponder and make their moves.

"Checkmate," said Max after five moves. "Sorry about that, Mr. Weinstock. I'm sure you'll beat me next time when we'll both have time to think through our moves more carefully."

Mr. Weinstock chuckled. "Yes, Max. I'm certain we'll *both* enjoy having more time for leisurely contemplation. Have a good day at school, dear."

"Thank you, sir."

Max hurried off, promising herself that, the next time they played, she'd definitely let Mr. Weinstock win.

Fortunately, her school was very close to Washington Square Park.

Because, even though she was only twelve, Max Einstein was already going to college—at New York University!

7

Phillip Stark watched the young girl running to school after her quick chess game with the old man in Washington Square Park.

It was hard to miss her. Her mop of curly hair bounced with every stride. Her trench coat flapped in the breeze behind her like a dirty pigeon's tail feathers.

She had to be the one.

The one who would earn Phillip Stark a tidy payday. The one whom, for whatever reason, the esteemed Dr. Zacchaeus Zimm was searching for, all over the globe.

Dr. Zimm had recently posted about this girl on webpages and chat groups frequented by those who shared Phillip Stark's unfortunate (although temporary) station in life as college teaching assistants. There was no photograph, just a very detailed description of the girl, including her love of chess. But Stark knew more about "Max Einstein" than Dr. Zimm.

Because she was in his class at New York University.

He also knew that if he orchestrated the delivery of this Einstein girl to Dr. Zimm, it would jump-start his career. He'd be set for life—doing the kind of theoretical research he knew he was always meant to do, especially given the size of his giant brain.

Dr. Zimm could give Stark anything he wanted. The famous professor had given up his prestigious professorship at a top-flight Ivy League college to head up a think tank for the Corp (that's what everybody called the shadowy group of multinational operators and oligarchs who, more or less, ruled the world). The Corp was extremely powerful and well-connected. They owned everything and everybody. If you scratched their back, they'd definitely scratch yours—probably with a thick wad of cash.

Stark made the call. The calm female voice on the other end of the phone urged him to stay in touch. He promised he would.

"When might I expect to hear from Dr. Zimm, himself?" he asked.

"We'll be in touch," said the lady.

"Perfect. By the way, you spell 'Stark' S-T—"

The lady hung up on him.

Probably because she was very busy. Soon, Stark would be busy, too. Working for Dr. Zimm.

Grinning, he hoped little Miss Einstein enjoyed today's lessons.

They would be her last.

8

Max hurried into an NYU building not far from Washington Square Park.

She found a seat in the back of the lecture hall. It was easier for a kid her age to slump down and remain semi-invisible in the rear of the room. Max had manipulated a few computer records (nobody really needed to know how) to create a realistic backstory for her attendance at the prestigious university. As far as the administrators at NYU were concerned, Maxine Einstein was a child prodigy, a genius like the character Sheldon Cooper on the *The Big Bang Theory*. It was the one TV show that Max actually enjoyed watching on YouTube.

She had borrowed (and improved on) a few ideas from the TV show. That's why her official college entrance records indicated that she graduated high school at the age of eleven after skipping most of elementary and middle school.

While she was at it, she also used her computer hacking skills to set up a few scholarships. She wasn't greedy. She just arranged for enough funding to cover tuition and books. Room and board, she took care of on her own—mostly by squatting in a foul-smelling room above a horse stable and eating lots of ramen noodles. Sometimes, when she was really craving egg rolls and cold noodles with sesame sauce, she also did deliveries for her favorite Chinese restaurant.

The Monday morning course at NYU was one of her favorites: 20th Century Concepts of Space, Time, & Matter. She was particularly interested in that day's lecture topic, "Schrödinger's Cat." It was a thought experiment developed in a bunch of back and forth letters between Einstein and Austrian physicist Erwin Schrödinger. Plus, it had a cat in it. Max liked cats.

Professor Burton's creepy graduate assistant, a twenty-something guy named Mr. Stark, came into the lecture hall and sort of leered at Max. Even though he was just a graduate student who helped the professor teaching the class, Stark dressed as if *he* were the professor, in a bow tie and a tweed sport jacket with patches on the elbows. He also sported a pair of thick, black-rimmed, smart-guy glasses.

"Ah, good morning, Miss Einstein," he said ghoulishly.

"Good morning, Mr. Stark."

He smirked and snapped open his fancy briefcase.

"I believe I have your mid-term exam," he said. "Ah, yes. Here it is. Tsk-tsk-tsk. You'd think someone named 'Einstein' would do better on a test about general relativity."

He handed Max a marked-up exam booklet with a big red "C" circled on the cover.

"Not much of a 'child prodigy,' are you?" he sneered.

Max lowered her eyes and wished that Mr. Stark would disappear. He didn't.

"Oh, I know all about child prodigies, Miss Einstein. They called me a genius when I was your age but my parents wouldn't let me skip grades. Thought it might prove socially awkward for me. So, they held me back. Kept me with kids my own age. Maybe your parents should've considered doing the same."

"Yes, sir," Max mumbled.

She tucked the exam booklet into her backpack. Of course, she could've aced the mid-term exam. In fact, it would've been easy for her to pull A's in *all* her classes at NYU. But she chose to maintain a solid C in all her course work, even if it meant she needed to answer a few exam questions incorrectly.

A "C" meant she was just an average student. Average students could fly undetected below the school administration's radar.

Or so she had always hoped.

Two burly men—who looked like college football players dressed in snug, black suits, white shirts, and skinny black ties—entered the lecture hall.

Max didn't recognize either of them. They weren't regular students in this class. Plus, not many NYU students wore black suits to class. They each had a miniature, curly-tailed communications device jammed into their ear.

"You Dr. Stark?" one of them asked the graduate assistant.

"Yes," said Mr. Stark, happy that the newcomers had mistaken him for a full professor.

"Where is she?"

Mr. Stark rolled his eyes. "Isn't it obvious, gentlemen? She's the only twelve-year-old girl currently sitting in this lecture hall."

He pointed at Max.

"I hope you enjoyed your time in college, Miss Einstein. Guess you'll be skipping this grade, too."

The two hulking men in black suits grabbed Max by the arms and hauled her out of her seat.

"You're coming with us."

9

"Do you gentlemen have badges?" Max asked as the brawny men dragged her toward the exit.

"We don't need badges," said the one holding Max's left arm.

Max didn't like that answer. "I find badges to be quite helpful for identifying—"

"Shut up, kid," said the one on her right. "We'll be the ones asking questions."

"We're with the New York City Administration for Children's Services," said the other one. "I'm Officer Jimenez. He's my partner, Officer Murphy."

"We know all about you," said Officer Murphy as the two men more or less shoved Max out to the street. "You go by the name of 'Max Einstein.' You have absolutely no business attending classes at NYU or any other college. You've been in and out of foster homes and orphanages your entire life. You have no known family. No birth certificate."

"How do you even know your name?" asked Officer Jimenez, who seemed angry at the world.

"I just always have," Max answered, meekly.

"Or maybe you just made it up," said Murphy.

The two large men were making Max very nervous, which was something that didn't happen very often. In fact, Max considered Fear and Worry to be wasted emotions. Max agreed with Dr. Einstein who once said, "I never worry about the future, it comes soon enough."

But these two NYC Children's Services officers were pushing Max's internal panic buttons.

If they really were officers.

Why wouldn't they show her their badges?

As they walked up the sidewalk toward an institutional white van (without any kind of official NYC government license plates), Max did some quick mental calculations. Employing the element of surprise while simultaneously factoring in the weight of her two captors, she figured she could definitely make a run for it. Because Newton's second law of motion said the rate of acceleration would depend on the mass of the objects attempting to move. Heavier objects (such as the two massive thugs gripping her arms) would speed up slower than lighter objects (such as Max).

Max blasted off, generating enough force to break free from her captors' grip.

"Hey, come back here!" shouted Jimenez.

Max ignored him and accelerated as rapidly as she could.

Across the street, she could see Washington Square Park. Maybe if she made it back to the chess tables and Mr. Weinstock, an adult, he could ask the questions the two goons clearly didn't want to hear from a twelve-year-old girl.

Max was about to bolt across the street.

When a bicycle going the wrong way cut her off.

The cyclist was texting while biking. He didn't swerve, didn't even see Max trying to dash across the street.

So *she* had to slam on her brakes and skid to a stop.

Which, of course, allowed the two extremely large gentlemen to gain momentum, catch up, and grab her.

This time, they lifted her feet off the street.

"That wasn't very smart, kid," said Murphy. "And you're supposed to be an Einstein?"

They hauled her back to the van.

"Where are you taking me?" she demanded.

"Little Angels," said Officer Jimenez. "It's a foster care

facility in Brooklyn. A safe place where we can keep an eye on you."

They loaded her into the back of the vehicle and locked the door.

"Mr. Kennedy will be worried," she said when the two men climbed into the van's front seats.

"Who's this Mr. Kennedy?" asked Murphy.

"A friend of mine. Can someone please tell him I'm okay?"

Officer Murphy stared at her for a beat in the rearview mirror.

Then he turned around and cranked the van's ignition.

"Nah, kid. We're not gonna do that. We're just gonna haul your butt to Brooklyn."

10

Max had been in foster care facilities like Brooklyn's Little Angels before.

She knew she could fit in if she had to.

She also knew that many foster care facilities were notoriously easy to escape from—once you worked out a foolproof plan. You just needed to prop a few pillows under the covers to make your cot look like somebody was sleeping in it when the staff shuffled around after midnight for bed check. It might take Max a few days to figure out the guards' routine but once she had it, she'd be heading back to Manhattan.

But not to the stables. She wouldn't want to get Mr. Kennedy and the others in trouble. No, she had to find someplace new and, somehow, make arrangements to retrieve her suitcase.

41

She couldn't lose it. The suitcase was the only thing in her whole mysterious life that tied her to some sort of history. The men in the suits were correct. She had no family. No birth certificate. The battered piece of luggage was her only link to her past.

Max and a nervous, blond boy named Quincy (who seemed terrified of everyone and everything) were sent to the Little Angels kitchen for "dinner prep."

The facility prided itself on "empowering children" by teaching them "practical kitchen skills and techniques."

That meant Max and Quincy had to put on aprons and peel potatoes if they wanted to eat potatoes for dinner. Max grabbed a potato peeler and went to work on the mountain of spuds sitting in the industrial sized sink.

Max glanced at Quincy. She really didn't know how to talk to kids. She'd never spent much time being one.

"I've never peeled potatoes before," said Quincy, who was very fidgety and twitchy. "Have you ever peeled potatoes?"

Max nodded. "Couple times."

A lot of foster care facilities taught "practical kitchen skills and techniques." It also meant they had to hire fewer cafeteria workers.

"Is there like a tab you peel back?" asked Quincy, fussing with a potato. "Like on a banana? I can peel a banana.

I had a banana for breakfast. I can peel an orange, too…"

Quincy was a mess. Max wanted to help him. So she summoned up all her courage and said, "Watch me."

She showed Quincy how to slide the peeler around the potato and make the curled skins drop into the waste barrel.

"You want to give it a go?" She held out the potato peeler.

Quincy eyed the thing as if it were a snake.

"I guess," he said. "I'm a little nervous around knives and blades and sharp things, you know? I cut myself once. I was slicing into a chocolate Easter bunny. The knife slipped. I nicked my knuckle. Needed six stitches. My foster family wasn't too happy. That's how I ended up here."

Max nodded. "I have a better idea. How about I peel the potatoes and you play with slime?"

"Slime?"

"Actually, it's a polymer. Not quite a solid, not quite a liquid, but very fun to play with."

"Cool."

Max scanned the kitchen cabinets and found a bottle of white glue, a box of borax laundry detergent, and some green food coloring. She mixed about a half of the glue bottle in a bowl with water and squirted in a few drops of green food coloring.

"That's just green glue," said Quincy.

43

"Hang on. Time for science."

She carefully added a tablespoon of the borax laundry detergent into the bowl and stirred slowly.

"Whoa!" said Quincy as Max pulled up a string of goopy sludge with her wooden spoon. "That's awesome."

"Knead it until it gets less sticky," said Max, passing the bowl over to Quincy. "Really work it around with your hands. We want the two compounds to bond."

Quincy happily squished the bowl of green slime.

Max peeled the potatoes and told Quincy stories about her time in the stables and all her friends there, including the horses.

The act of squeezing and massaging the slime while listening to Max's stories seemed to soothe Quincy. He stopped fidgeting and concentrated on the gooey task at hand.

Max finished prepping the pile of potatoes.

"Quincy? Two more things. Number one: be sure to wash your hands before dinner."

"No problem. What's number two?"

"Don't put that bowl of slime anywhere near the dinner table. People might think it's some kind of mystery vegetable."

"Yeah," said Quincy. "It kind of looks like the spinach they served last night. It was super slimy, too!"

11

Max huddled down on a cot in the room she shared with five other girls whose names she didn't know. There wasn't much point in making friends. Max didn't plan on staying at Little Angels for more than a day or so.

Two of her roommates were snoring like motorcycles with clogged carburetors. Max, on the other hand, couldn't fall asleep. She missed her books. Her computer. Her Einstein memorabilia.

She missed her friends at the stable and hoped they weren't worrying about her too much.

She was so alone.

All she had were the thoughts flickering through her mind. And, as always, she had about a billion of those.

So, she did what she typically did on nights when sleep

wouldn't come: she struck up a conversation with Albert Einstein. It was all in her head, of course. Nothing too kooky. Max didn't actually *see* Albert Einstein sitting in a chair in the corner or floating above her bed, puffing on his pipe.

With Max, it was more or less an old-school Socratic debate with herself. That meant she taught herself the way the ancient Greek philosopher Socrates taught his pupils: by asking and answering questions.

"So, I have a question about the theory of relativity," she thought to herself.

"Excellent," replied the gentle voice of Albert Einstein in her head. "One of my favorite subjects."

"It explains so much."

"Thank you."

"But if everything is relative, how can you know what's actually true?"

"Ah! Easy. It's *all* true. It's just relative to your perspective."

"What about this whole 'time dilation' thing? How can time expand?"

"Also easy. Time is simply another form of measurement. If you're on a rocket ship zooming through space, time won't feel any different to you inside your space capsule. But the measurement of time would be different if taken on earth, which isn't moving nearly as rapidly as you and your spaceship. If you traveled at near light speed to a distant planet, by the time you returned to earth, thousands of years might have passed here. Yet only a few years will have ticked away inside your space vessel."

"That's wild."

"That's the universe."

The mental discussion was having the desired effect. Max was starting to feel drowsy. She stifled a yawn and asked her inner Einstein one last question.

"Okay, your most famous equation, $E=mc^2$, means that the energy of something is equal to its mass—the amount of matter it has—times the speed of light *squared*."

"Correct."

"But when you square the speed of light—when you multiply one hundred and eighty-six thousand miles per second times one hundred and eighty-six thousand miles per second—you end up with a huge number!"

"Indeed, you do. Approximately thirty-four billion, five-hundred-and-ninety-six million."

"So that means that even the tiniest object contains an enormous amount of energy, right?"

"Bingo. Even the smallest among us have the potential to add a gigantic amount of energy to this world. And if you don't believe that, first thing tomorrow morning, just look in the mirror."

And, with a smile on her face, Max finally fell asleep.

12

Early the next morning, after rising at six to cook a huge vat of oatmeal and learn some more valuable kitchen skills (like how to stir twenty pounds of mush with a wooden spoon the size of a boat oar), Max was informed that she would be going to school.

"NYU?" she asked eagerly.

"No," the stern matron replied. "You're twelve years old, correct?"

"Yes, ma'am."

"Then you belong in middle school. With all the other twelve-year-old boys and girls."

"B-b-but…"

The matron gave her an icy look. Max took the hint. She quit protesting.

Of course, it was totally ridiculous for the powers that be at the Little Angels foster care facility to insist that she go to a "regular" school. Max may have been young and somewhat small, but she had all that unlimited potential and mental energy bottled up inside her. (Just ask Dr. Einstein!)

Besides, she had finished everything the seventh grade had to teach her about math and science when she was seven years old. She had found an old textbook in a thrift shop when she was young. There was a big "7" on the cover. Max had thought it meant you were supposed to learn the material between the covers when you were seven years old.

So, she did.

"Shake a leg," said the driver as Max and all the other foster kids between the ages of eleven and fourteen piled into the van heading for the nearest Brooklyn middle school.

Max went to the classes she was supposed to go to.

She didn't say a word during English, or math, or social studies.

In science, she focused on a dusty shaft of sunlight that streamed through a window and illuminated her desk like a heavenly spotlight.

What would it be like, she thought, *to ride that beam of light?*

Legend had it that this was how Albert Einstein first

started contemplating his theory of relativity. He was riding a bicycle, saw a sunbeam, and let his mind wander. *What would it be like to ride beside a sunbeam to the edge of the universe?*

Max knew that daydreams (the kind that Mr. Kennedy teased her about) often led to the most important scientific discoveries. So she drifted off. She chased that dusty sunbeam out the window. She followed it through space and time. This was what Dr. Einstein used to call a thought experiment—ideas that he played with in his mind instead of a laboratory.

Maybe it was the trancelike nature of the thought experiment.

Or the fact that Max had had so much difficulty drifting off to sleep the night before.

Or the warmth of the sunshine on her face.

But as she chased that beam in her brain, her eyes grew heavy. The shaft of quivering light felt warm and cozy beside her. The universe was lulling her to sleep.

Suddenly, far off, somewhere in the dark distance, near the edge of the universe, Max heard someone calling her name.

"Miss Einstein? Miss Einstein?"

This was followed by the bang of a wooden ruler against a desk.

Speed of
light =
186,000
miles per
second.
You have
to pedal
very fast.

The teacher.

Max had fallen asleep in class.

A bell rang. It was definitely time for Max to wake up. It was also time for her to move on to her next class.

But first she apologized to the teacher.

"I'm sorry, sir," she told him. "I didn't mean any disrespect. Sometimes my mind wanders off and I need to chase after it."

"Not in my classroom you don't," said the teacher. "Here we stay focused and memorize the answers to the questions we know will be on the state science test. Do I make myself clear, Miss Einstein?"

"Yes, sir."

The teacher looked at her suspiciously. "Einstein. Is that really your name?"

"Yes," said Max because, as far as she knew, she was telling the truth.

"Any relation?"

"To Dr. Albert Einstein?"

"No," said the teacher sarcastically. "The brothers who bake the bagels."

"Not to my knowledge, sir."

The teacher waved her off. "Memorize the formulae in chapter three by tomorrow. And don't you dare fall asleep in my classroom again, young lady!"

"Yes, sir. I mean, no, sir."

Max stuck to herself and muddled through the rest of her school day. At dismissal time, the beat-up van from Little Angels was waiting out front to pick up Max and the other middle schoolers.

Once again, she thought about making a run for it.

There had to be a subway station close by. Max could race back to the stables, grab her suitcase, and search out a new place to sleep. She could find a new college to attend, too. Columbia University, way uptown, had some excellent courses for her to choose from. She couldn't stand the idea of being stuck in a seventh-grade classroom, memorizing facts and figures by rote.

She couldn't just go along to get along.

Max took in a deep breath. She was ready to bolt.

But if the men in the suits ever found out about the stables, they could make life difficult for Mr. Kennedy and Mrs. Rabinowitz.

She realized she would be better off going with her original plan. Sneaking out after dark. She just needed to observe and chart the late-night routines of the security staff for a few more days. She could handle a few more days. Time was on her side.

She climbed into the van with the rest of the crowd. Max sat in the back, so she wouldn't have to chit-chat with any of the kids. Max didn't chit or chat very well.

When they arrived back at the foster care facility, Max received some very unexpected news.

She had visitors.

13

"Your visitors are in my office," said Mrs. Groober, the woman in charge of the Little Angels foster care facility. "Please make this visit brief. I would like my office back."

"Yes, ma'am."

Max stepped into the room.

And her jaw dropped.

"Mr. Weinstock?"

It was her chess buddy from Washington Square Park.

"Yes, indeed," he replied in his plummy English accent.

Max was confused. What was Mr. Weinstock doing at her foster care facility? And who were the young man and woman waiting with him? They both had dark hair, interesting eyes, and olive complexions. They were also extremely good looking and athletic. They could've been fashion models, for sure.

"Ah, where are my manners?" said Mr. Weinstock. "Allow me to introduce Charl and Isabl."

When he said the names, they sounded like "Sharl" and "Is-bull."

"Charl and Isabl, this is Max Einstein."

The young man and woman stood up to shake Max's hand.

Max took a step back. Charl and Isabl weren't wearing black suits or skinny black ties but, after her run-in with the officers who yanked her out of NYU, she was a little leery around strange characters she'd never met before.

"We're the good guys, Miss Einstein," said the man named Charl, with an accent that Max couldn't quite place.

"They are, Max," said Mr. Weinstock. "In fact, they are the *very* good guys. The best. Unfortunately, there are others who…well, we don't have time for all that, now. But, believe me, dear, Charl and Isabl are here to help."

Max took the young man's outstretched hand. "Thank you, Mister…"

Charl smiled. "No last name. Just Charl."

"And I'm just Isabl," said the lady, who also had an accent. "We find it easier to do our work if we stay on a first-name-only basis. It helps us stay one step ahead of the Corp."

"What's the Corp?" asked Max.

Mr. Weinstock grimaced. "Those would be the bad guys I was going to mention earlier."

"Maxine," said Isabl, "we represent the CMI."

"The who?"

"The Change Makers Institute."

Okay, thought Max. *CMI sounds impressive. Like the FBI, CIA, or KGB.* So far, she liked the CMI much better than the Corp. After all, the Institute hadn't hauled her out of a college classroom or chased her into a city street where a distracted bicyclist was riding the wrong way.

She kept listening.

"We've been studying you for quite some time," said Charl. "Your file. Your records."

Max had a file and records? Who knew?

"So have others," added Isabl.

"The Corp?" asked Max.

All three adults nodded.

"Mr. Weinstock's been keeping an eye on you for us," said Isabl. "He is the one who alerted us to your current... situation."

"You mean my run-in with the law?"

"They weren't the law," said Charl. "They were paid mercenaries, hired by Dr. Zacchaeus Zimm."

"Who's he?"

Isabl glanced at her watch. "We'll explain over dinner."

"You guys are going to eat here with us tonight?" said Max. "If so, you might want to stay away from the mystery meat…"

"We can't stay here," said Isabl.

"We're taking you out to dinner, Max," said Mr. Weinstock.

"Oh-kay. Can I ask a question?"

"Make it brief," said Isabl, who really had a thing about watching her watch.

"Why?"

Charl and Isabl paused and looked intently at each other before turning to Max.

"Simple," said Charl. "We've talked to your professors at NYU. Your classmates. We are unbelievably impressed with you." Then he smiled. "The only thing more difficult than getting top grades in college is getting a precisely calibrated C average," he added, knowingly.

"You might just be our top candidate," said Isabl.

"Really?" said Max. "For what?"

"We want you to come to Jerusalem with us."

"It's a great honor, Max," said Mr. Weinstock. "A once in a lifetime opportunity."

"We leave tonight at eight fifty-four," said Charl.

"But what about school?" asked Max.

58

"You'll be attending a new school. Very different than any you have ever attended—even NYU."

"It's more experiential," said Isabl. "You'll *do* things. We suspect it will prove much more suitable for a mind such as yours."

"But it's in Jerusalem?" said Max.

"Yes," said Isabl. "You'll find out more once you get there. We must leave. Now. The others won't be far behind us."

"The, uh, others?"

Charl nodded. "The men in the black suits."

14

Max looked to Mr. Weinstock.

Even without parents, Max knew she shouldn't accept plane rides from total strangers. Especially not to foreign destinations. She probably shouldn't even go out to dinner with them. She needed someone she trusted to tell her this was a smart and safe idea.

"To be chosen by the CMI is a great honor, Max," Mr. Weinstock repeated softly. "A rare opportunity. They can protect you from Dr. Zimm and the Corp."

Max played the mental game she sometimes played when she needed to make a major decision: "What would Einstein do?"

In a flash, her hero's words came swirling back to her:

"Wisdom is not a product of schooling but of the lifelong attempt to acquire it."

"Okay," said Max. "Let's go. But, first, I need to pick up my suitcase. It's at the stables."

"Fine," said Charl. "After dinner, we will retrieve it."

He gestured toward the door.

"We have an early reservation at Le Bernardin," said Isabl, giving her watch yet another check.

"The finest restaurant in all of New York!" beamed Mr. Weinstock. "A marvelous choice for a celebration. I trust you enjoy seafood, Maxine?"

"It's okay, I guess. But I was wondering—would it be possible to go out for Chinese instead?"

"We can discuss this in the car," said Isabl. "We have to hurry. Dr. Zimm himself is coming down from Boston."

"Who's he again?"

"Someone you do not want to meet, dear," said Mr. Weinstock.

Max hustled out of the office with the three adults.

"Are you leaving?"

Mrs. Groober was standing in the Little Angels lobby, her hands firmly planted on her hips. She made a very formidable roadblock.

"Yes," said Mr. Weinstock, tipping his cap. "Thank you

for your hospitality and the use of your office, Mrs. Groober. Frightfully kind."

"Have a good evening," said the stern woman, who had the bearing of a prison warden. "Maxine? You're needed in the kitchen. Those carrots aren't going to peel themselves."

Max was about to say, "Yes, ma'am," when Charl and Isabl each took one of her hands.

"Maxine won't be staying for dinner," said Charl.

"She's coming home with us, Mrs. Groober," said Isabl.

"Is that so?"

"Yes. We are adopting her."

"You'll find all the necessary paperwork in your office," said Mr. Weinstock. His English accent made him sound very authoritative. "You'll also find the signed and notarized OCFS-4156 and UCS-836 forms on your desk. I trust you'll find everything in order." Now he sounded extremely lawyerly. "Good day, Mrs. Groober. We're off to celebrate the creation of a new and happy family. Thank you for all you have done to make this cherished moment possible."

Mrs. Groober went into her office to search for the adoption documents, which, of course, she would never find.

"Run," Charl and Isabl whispered to Max.

"Indeed," added Mr. Weinstock.

The four of them scurried out the door and tumbled

into a black sedan with tinted windows that was parked at the curb.

Isabl got behind the wheel. Charl took the front passenger seat. Mr. Weinstock and Max sat in the back.

"I'd buckle up if I were you," Mr. Weinstock suggested.

Max did.

Right before Isabl rocketed the car away from the curb in a tire-squealing, rubber-burning blastoff.

Max white-knuckled her overhead handhold as the vehicle zoomed from zero to way-too-fast in a nanosecond.

"Do you always drive like a maniac?" She shouted because it was the only way to be heard over the roaring engine.

"Only when necessary," said Isabl, tugging the steering wheel hard to the right to careen the car around a tight corner.

Max heard a shrill phone chirrup.

"Dr. Zimm just landed," said Charl, studying the face of his glowing phone. "He'll be at Little Angels soon."

"I hope he enjoys stewed carrots," laughed Mr. Weinstock as Isabl put the speedy sedan through its gear-shifting paces. "We, on the other hand, are going out for Chinese. Isn't that correct, Max?"

And, for the first time all day, Max smiled. "Yes, sir. But I think we better get it to go."

15

Dr. Zimm was furious.

"Where is she?" he demanded, forcing his face into a smile. His teeth looked too big for his mouth.

"She left," said Mrs. Groober. "About half an hour ago. An elderly man with an English accent and two young foreigners took her."

Dr. Zimm arched an eyebrow that made his forehead furrow all the way up to his cleanly shaved dome. "By any chance were their names Charl and Isabl?"

"They didn't give me their names. They simply said they were adopting the girl."

"Is that so?" seethed Dr. Zimm. "Tell me, Mrs. Groober. Do you typically adopt out children to people whose names you do not know?"

Mrs. Groober was about to answer when Dr. Zimm held up his gloved hand. It was black, just like his suitcoat and slender necktie. "That was a rhetorical question, Mrs. Groober. Meaning I do not expect or want you to answer it."

Mrs. Groober smiled coyly. "I hope this slight glitch will not affect the terms of our financial understanding?"

Dr. Zimm tugged down on his sleek leather gloves. The two men in black suits and sunglasses flanking him inched forward toward the matron. Both men wore earpieces but they weren't using them. They didn't need to. They were taking their orders directly from Dr. Zimm.

"If the money is an issue," said Mrs. Groober, her voice quavering with fear, "we could renegotiate the particulars…"

Dr. Zimm did not answer the woman's question about money. He didn't have time. He knew his rivals from the CMI had at least half an hour jump on him.

They also had the Einstein girl.

The one Dr. Zimm desperately needed for the Corp.

But where would Charl and Isabl take the girl genius?

Dr. Zimm did the mental calculus. His minions had, on a tip from the NYU teaching assistant, picked up Miss Einstein at a college lecture hall. They had delivered her to the Little Angels foster care facility for safekeeping until Dr. Zimm could personally pick the girl up.

That meant the girl had been snatched away with only

the clothes on her back and whatever items she took to class that day. Her instinct would be to rush back to where she'd been living (or hiding) so she could gather up whatever meager personal belongings she might possess.

That's where Dr. Zimm and his associates could grab her. Charl, Isabl, and some old man with an English accent would be no match for Dr. Zimm and his two heavily armed, commando-trained companions.

"Tell me, Mrs. Groober," he asked, "did the girl have any friends here at your…facility?"

"She was here for such a short time…"

"Did she have any interactions at all? Someone she may have spoken with?"

"Well," said Mrs. Groober, pondering the question. "Last night. She was on kitchen duty with a young boy named Quincy. He's a nervous, fidgety type. As skittish as a kitten."

Dr. Zimm grinned. "And where is this boy, now?"

"In his room."

"Take us there."

"B-b-but…"

"Unless, of course, you want me to suspend my generous contribution to the great work you, personally, are doing here?"

Mrs. Groober blinked. "Quincy's in Room 202 with some of the other boys. It's this way."

Dr. Zimm and his two associates followed Mrs. Groober down the dim hallway. They let her get about ten feet in front of them so they could communicate in hushed whispers.

"Mr. Jimenez?" Dr. Zimm said to the black-suited man on his left.

"Yes, sir?"

"Once we have Miss Einstein in custody, please visit the teaching assistant who helped arrange her transport to this safe house."

"Mr. Stark?"

"Precisely. He is a loose end. And what do we do with loose ends?"

Jimenez grinned. "We send them to the special places."

"Precisely. Greenland. Siberia. Devil's Island. Kindly initiate an appropriate relocation package for Mr. Stark, immediately."

"What about Mrs. Groober, there?" asked the other out of the side of his mouth.

Dr. Zimm sighed. "Alas, Mr. Murphy, she is another loose end in need of tying. Might I suggest our facility in the Sahara Desert?"

Murphy rolled his thick neck. Several vertebrae cracked.

"We'll take care of it, doc," he said.

Dr. Zimm smiled. "I'm certain you will, Mr. Murphy. I'm certain you will."

16

"**Are you sure you wouldn't prefer the cuisine at Le** Bernardin?" asked Mr. Weinstock. "It is top rated in the city."

"The Mee Noodle Shop is awesome," Max told Mr. Weinstock as everyone started piling out of the parked sedan. Her restaurant choice looked a little shabby and run-down. "This is a neighborhood fave."

"Perhaps. But is it *sanitary?*" Mr. Weinstock's English accent made him sound super snooty.

Max tapped the grade "A" sign from the NYC Health Department posted in the restaurant's front window.

"It's super clean," she said. "So we have nothing to worry about."

"Except Dr. Zimm," mumbled Charl.

"I doubt he'll be searching for us...*here,*" sniffed Mr. Weinstock.

"I'm sorry this isn't the best restaurant in New York," said Max, sensing her friend's disappointment. "But they have seafood here, too. Scallops, shrimp, salmon..."

"Oh, joy."

"Hiya, Max," said the host who greeted the group inside the restaurant. "Table for four?"

"No thanks, Mr. Lin. We need to get this order to go."

Max and Mr. Lin were friendly. From time to time, during the dinner rush, she'd hop on one of the restaurant's bikes and help with deliveries. Her paycheck always came in a cardboard takeout container: free food for dinner. (She also got to keep her tips!)

Mr. Lin pulled out a stubby pencil and order pad. "What would you folks like?"

"Let's see," said Max, calling up the restaurant's menu from memory. "Scallion pancakes, two orders of pan-fried dumplings, crispy chicken in sesame sauce...three of those. Three General Tso's chicken, too. A couple lo meins with shrimp, stir-fried rice..."

She ordered three dozen different dishes.

"How about you guys?" she asked the others. "You want anything?"

"Um, no thanks," said Isabl. "What you ordered should be plenty for all of us."

"Oh, I'm sorry. This food isn't for me. It's for my friends."

"Pardon?" said Mr. Weinstock.

"Mr. Kennedy, Mrs. Rabinowitz, Roxanne, Pablo…the whole gang at the stables. They haven't had a good Chinese dinner since forever."

"Oh," said Charl. "In that case, double everything, Mr. Lin."

Mr. Lin looked at his order pad. He also looked stunned. "Will you be paying for this with a credit card?" he asked.

"No," said Isabl. "Cash."

She reached into a zippered pocket on her sleek leather jacket and extracted several one-hundred-dollar bills. She handed the money to Mr. Lin.

"This is too much," said Mr. Lin.

"You forgot to factor in the tip," said Charl with a smile.

Mr. Lin bowed quickly and dashed off to the kitchen.

"Lesson number one," Charl said to Max. "Credit cards leave a trail. Always carry cash."

"Thank you," said Max. "But, uh, I don't have any cash…"

"At the CMI," said Isabl, "you will be given a comfortable allowance. Provided, of course, you do your chores."

When the food was ready, Max and her new friends

loaded a dozen shopping bags filled with steaming, fragrant Chinese food takeout containers into the trunk and backseat of the car.

They cruised a few blocks west and south to the stables.

"We're taking note of this," said Charl.

"Of what?" asked Max, genuinely confused.

"Your generosity," said Charl.

"It is an excellent trait," added Isabl. "We offered you a celebration for yourself. You turned it into a feast for others."

"Well, I'm still not exactly sure what we're celebrating, but what fun is a party if you don't invite your friends and neighbors?"

Isabl parked the car in front of the stables.

She and Charl announced that they would be staying with the vehicle while Max and Mr. Weinstock toted the food up the steps to the third floor.

"We need to be ready to initiate a rapid extraction protocol should any unanticipated company attempt to crash your party," said Charl.

"You're still worried about this Dr. Zimm?" asked Max.

"Constantly," said Isabl.

"But we shan't let that, or anything else, ruin your bon voyage celebration, Maxine," said Mr. Weinstock, grabbing hold of a dozen different bag handles. "Lead the way."

Mr. Kennedy emerged from the shadows.

"Max?" he said. "What's goin' on? Did you win the lottery, girl?"

"No," said Max with a laugh. "My new friends and I just wanted to treat you guys to Chinese tonight!"

"That's a mighty fancy car you're driving around in, too," said Mr. Kennedy.

"Yeah," said Max. "And Isabl there, behind the wheel? She drives it like a maniac."

"Did you bring bagels, Max?" asked Mrs. Rabinowitz, coming out of the stables to check out all the commotion.

"Not tonight, Mrs. Rabinowitz. But I picked up your favorites from the noodle shop. Moo goo gai pan with brown rice with a side order of egg rolls."

Mrs. Rabinowitz bounced up and down on her heels and clapped. "Forget the bagels. I'll have leftover Chinese food for breakfast."

"What's the occasion, Max?" asked Mr. Kennedy, taking charge of a half-dozen bags and leading the way into the stables, which still reeked of horse manure.

"Well, sir, I'm going on a trip."

"Is that so?"

"Yes. I'll need my suitcase."

"Uhm-hmm. Going someplace special?"

"Very," said Mr. Weinstock. "But we'd rather not discuss the details."

"And why's that, Mister…?"

"Einstein," said Mr. Weinstock, smoothly. "Mr. Leonard Einstein. I'm Maxine's long-lost uncle. She's coming home with me."

"Well, I'll be darned," said Mr. Kennedy. "Chinese food and a long-lost uncle. This is your lucky day, ain't it, Max?"

"I hope so, Mr. Kennedy. I hope so."

17

Working on information they were able to obtain from the boy, Quincy, Dr. Zimm and his associates arrived at the stables on the west side of Manhattan.

Thirty-four minutes after Max and her companions had already left.

"Where did she go?" Dr. Zimm asked Mr. Kennedy, who was being physically restrained by Mr. Murphy and Mr. Jimenez.

"To her uncle's place," said Mr. Kennedy.

Then he belched. His breath smelled of garlic shrimp and cold noodles swimming in peanut sauce.

"And where is that?" demanded Dr. Zimm. His large teeth and pinched-tight skin made him look like a bald skull with eyeballs. "Where is her uncle's place?"

"Not one hundred percent sure," said Mr. Kennedy.

Dr. Zimm nodded at Mr. Murphy and Mr. Jimenez. They tightened their grips on Mr. Kennedy's arms.

"Whoa. Ease up, there, brother…"

"Tell me what I need to know, Mr. Kennedy, and my associates will immediately loosen their grips," said Dr. Zimm. "We have no interest in hurting you. We simply need to find the girl."

"Why? Who's she to you?"

Dr. Zimm grinned. "One of my lost sheep."

"Huh?"

Dr. Zimm waved the homeless man off. "Miss Einstein is a very valuable asset. She represents an incredible investment of time and money—"

"You know Max?"

Dr. Zimm pursed his lips. He'd already said more than he should have.

He forced another smile onto his face. "I intend to offer Maxine an amazing opportunity."

Mr. Kennedy eyed him suspiciously. "Is that right?"

"Indeed so. A mind such as Miss Einstein's should not be wasted here, hiding in a horse stable or gallivanting around the country with her 'family.'" He said the word as if he didn't believe the man who took Max away from the stables was in any way related to her. "Now then, I will ask you one more time, Mr. Kennedy: Where did Maxine's 'uncle' take her?"

"Like I told you, mister. I don't know."

"Fine." He turned to Jimenez. "Go grab the old lady, Mrs. Rabinowitz. Maybe, with some encouragement, her memory will prove sharper than Mr. Kennedy's."

"Wait," said Kennedy. "Hang on. I might be remembering something here. Yeah. Milwaukee."

"I beg your pardon?" said Dr. Zimm, his eyes sparkling.

"It just came back to me. Her uncle took her to Milwaukee."

"Is that so?"

"Definitely, man. See, I was enjoying some cold noodles with sesame sauce and Peking duck. The uncle, Mr. Einstein, he says, 'Oh, just you wait until you taste the Chinese food back home in Milwaukee, Max. It's even better than what you folks have here in New York.'"

Mr. Murphy let go of Kennedy's arm and whipped out a phone. He swiped and tapped the screen.

"There's a nine thirty-three direct flight to Milwaukee out of Newark, New Jersey," he reported. "If we hurry, we can make it."

"Thank you for your assistance, Mr. Kennedy," said Dr. Zimm. "If I were you, I would forget all about our brief encounter."

"Oh, don't you worry," said Mr. Kennedy. "I already have. In fact, I don't think you and I have ever met."

"Excellent. One more thing."

"What's that?"

"If we don't find Max in Milwaukee, remember this: we know how to find you."

18

Isabl drove (under the speed limit) to a private air-field in New Jersey.

Max could see small corporate jets parked on the far side of a chain-link fence topped with coils of barbed wire.

"So, I guess we're not flying to Jerusalem on one of the major airlines, huh?" she said.

"We need to fly you in under the radar," said Charl from the front of the car.

That made Max shiver a little. Flying under the radar would mean doing something called nap-of-the-earth avia-tion (or NOE)—a type of very low-altitude flying used by military aircraft to avoid detection by the enemy's radar sen-sors. It's also called "ground-hugging" or "hedgehopping."

It means you're flying just above the treetops!

Max had never flown before,

She didn't want her first flight to be through a tangle of tree branches.

"It's just a figure of speech, dear," said Mr. Weinstock, reading the terrified look on Max's face. "Under the radar means we want as few people as possible to know that you are anywhere near Jerusalem or the CMI."

Isabl motored the car up the gravel drive. Security gates parted smoothly as she approached.

"We are expected," she said.

A man who looked like a soldier in a dark-green flight suit marched up to Isabl's window. She rolled it down.

"Your flight plan has been filed and approved with the IDF," said the military man. He handed Isabl an iPad shielded in a thick plastic case. It looked bulletproof.

"Thank you, Lieutenant," said Isabl, driving the car toward an open hangar, where Max could see a glistening white jet bathed in brilliant light. A motorcycle with a side-car was parked next to it.

"What's the IDF?" asked Max, who was curious about everything.

"Israel Defense Forces," said Charl. "They will be expecting us."

"Excellent," said Mr. Weinstock. "Unexpected visitors

in Israeli airspace are often greeted by fighter jets. Have a safe flight and a productive journey, Max."

Isabl parked the car. Everyone piled out. Mr. Weinstock went over to the motorcycle.

"This is where I leave you, Max," he said. "I will miss our chess games together."

"You're not coming with us?" she asked.

Mr. Weinstock shook his head. "You don't need me any longer. You have Charl and Isabl. And, of course, the CMI. You have been chosen."

"What exactly have I been chosen for?"

"Patience, dear. All shall be revealed later, when it's safe."

"But first," said Isabl, "we need to fly to Jerusalem."

"Is that guy in the flight suit our pilot?" Max nodded toward the front gate.

"No. He's part of our ground crew."

"So, um, when do the pilots show up?"

"We're already here," said Charl. "I'll take the first seat for wheels up. Isabl will take over for the landing."

"You guys are pilots, too?"

"Yes," said Isabl.

Max felt a little queasy. She hoped Isabl didn't fly the same way she drove.

Mr. Weinstock was straddling the motorcycle and strapping on a helmet.

"I'm going to circle back to the stables," he announced. "I'll make certain Dr. Zimm didn't do any irreparable harm when he visited your friends."

Max was shocked. "Dr. Zimm went to the stables?"

"We hope he didn't," said Mr. Weinstock, "but we must assume that he did or that he eventually will. Not to worry. I have the keys to several lovely apartments for your squatter friends to move into this very night. Our benefactor has paid their rent for a full year."

"Seriously?" said Max.

"Seriously."

"Well, who's this benefactor? I want to thank him."

"Perhaps, at a later date, you two will meet and you'll be able to thank him in person." Mr. Weinstock pulled on his motorcycle helmet. "Enjoy the flight, Max. Do well and do good. Make the world a better place." He gave a hearty wave and puttered off into the night.

Happy that Mr. Kennedy, Mrs. Rabinowitz, and the rest would be moving into real apartments, Max was practically skipping as she followed Charl and Isabl up the steep metal stairs into the private jet.

"We'll be up front in the cockpit," said Charl.

"That means the entire cabin is yours," added Isabl.

"There's food and beverages in the galley," Charl continued. "Help yourself to anything you'd like—once we reach a comfortable cruising altitude and I turn off the fasten seat belt sign. And try to get some sleep. It's a ten-and-a-half-hour flight. You'll need to hit the ground running when we land in Jerusalem. The others have already arrived."

"The others?" said Max. "What others?"

Isabl smiled. "All will be explained. Later."

Later.

That seemed to be when a lot of stuff was going to happen.

"This whole thing doesn't make much sense," she said. "And why is this Dr. Zimm after me? I don't even know any doctors named Zimm…"

Charl sighed. "Please be patient, Maxine. You'll understand everything—"

"Later, right?"

"Right."

19

Max made her way into the main cabin.

It smelled brand new. She couldn't believe how soft and cushiony the leather chairs were. And they reclined! Plus, there were all sorts of plump pillows and fleecy blankets. Her seat would be the most comfortable bed she'd slept in for years.

She took a seat near a window.

It was her first time flying. She wanted to enjoy the view.

She wondered if her hero, Albert Einstein, had ever flown in a plane. Probably not. In all of the biographies she'd read, his trips around the world—to the United States, South America, and even Japan—had been by ship. He didn't travel a lot after he got older and started doing research and giving lectures in Princeton, New Jersey. So, Max was pretty confident she was about to do something her hero had never done!

Max also knew that one of Professor Einstein's biggest flops had to do with airplanes. In 1916, he wrote a technical article proposing a new shape for airplane wings. He wanted to, basically, put a hump in the middle. He theorized it would help the airplane generate lift, the force that pulled the wings up from the earth as air flowed over them. Intrigued, German engineers built a full-size prototype of his idea—a World War I biplane with double "Einstein wings" attached.

The test pilot took off and landed almost immediately. The plane with the humped wings was hard to control, he reported. "It waddled while flying," he said, "mimicking the flight of a pregnant duck."

Einstein accepted the failure of his humped wing design with his usual good humor, writing, "That is what can happen to a man who thinks a lot, but reads little."

Einstein always embraced his failures. It was something Max had tried to do, too. Because, like her hero said, "Only one who does not question is safe from making a mistake."

Charl taxied the small jet to the end of the runway.

Distance from
New York to Jerusalem:
5660 miles (9109 kilometers)

Travel time by plane: <u>10.5 hours</u>
Travel time by boat and train: <u>15 days</u>

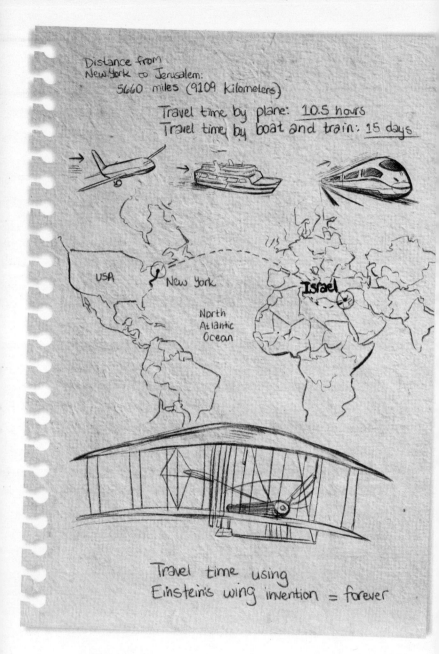

Travel time using
Einstein's wing invention = forever

"We are number one for takeoff," he announced through the PA speaker. "See you in Israel, Max!"

The plane powered down the long strip and gracefully lifted off.

Max could see the twinkling lights of Manhattan. She studied the familiar landmarks and pinpointed the location of the stables, so near to the edge of the Hudson River.

Her friends were all getting new homes. So was she. Hers would be lot farther away from the stables than theirs.

"This is amazing!" she said out loud as the plane cleared the Statue of Liberty and passed over the necklace of tiny lights holding up the massive Verrazano-Narrows Bridge at the mouth of New York Harbor.

In a matter of minutes, they were soaring across the night sky, high above the Atlantic Ocean, heading east to Israel.

Max knew she should close her eyes and go to sleep.

But she was too excited. The whole day had been so magical. And scary. And exhilarating.

Charl and Isabl seemed nice. And smart. And super skilled. *Was there anything those two didn't know how to do?* She liked them. They seemed to like her. But they were, basically, total strangers—endorsed by another semi-stranger, Mr. Weinstock.

Now Max was turning her whole life upside down because this trio of strangers had told her she needed to go to Jerusalem and join something called the CMI, even though none of them would tell her why. Sometimes, Max wished she had a real friend. Maybe someone her own age. Someone she could talk about stuff with. Someone who might understand how she was feeling because they sometimes felt that same way, too.

"Please be patient," Charl had said. *"You'll understand everything…later."*

Everything?

Did Charl and Isabl know who Max was? Did they know how she got her last name? Did they know her parents?

Is that what this is all about?

Max certainly hoped so.

As the jet glided through the starlit night, Max closed her eyes and initiated another conversation with the Albert Einstein in her head.

"When will it be later?" she asked.

"Time is relative and flexible," came the reply. "The dividing line between past, present, and future is an illusion—although a convincing one."

"So, I have to wait forever to find the answers to all my questions?"

"The wait only seems long, Max, because you are so eager to learn the answers. That's relativity."

"Huh?"

"Put your hand on a hot stove for a minute and it seems like an hour. Sit with a cute boy for an hour and it seems like a minute."

Max blushed and changed the subject. She didn't have time for cute boys.

She had to fly to Israel and, hopefully, find out who she really was!

20

The private jet landed at Ben Gurion International Airport in Tel Aviv, where it was met by a windowless white van near a private hangar.

"Is this the girl?" asked a gruff woman with a thick German accent waiting beside the van. She looked to be fifty-some years old with no-nonsense hair and a stiff military bearing.

"Yes, Tari," said Isabl.

"She doesn't look all that special," said the unsmiling woman as she sized up Max. Max was wearing a brand-new navy-blue tracksuit she had found wrapped in plastic in the cabin of the private jet. There was a "CMI" stitched into the chest.

"Max is quite a find, I assure you, Tari," said Charl.

90

"One we have been working on for years. Rest assured, her presence at the CMI will add a great deal to our efforts."

Max smiled at the unsmiling woman. "I can't wait to see what kind of awesome stuff you guys are up to, Tari."

"You are to address me as 'Ms. Kaplan' at all times. Do you understand?"

"Yes, ma'am, Ms. Kaplan. I'm Max. Max Einstein."

"So Charl and Isabl have informed me. Tell me, Miss *Einstein*—is that a pseudonym? A name you decided to give yourself? Or maybe it is simply some kind of American joke?"

"No, ma'am. It's just my name. The only one I can remember, anyway."

"It is also a name we should not broadcast too loudly or widely," said Isabl. "Dr. Zimm has ears everywhere."

Ms. Kaplan's whole expression changed. It went from skeptical to terrified in a flash.

"So, the rumors are true?"

Charl and Isabl nodded.

"What rumors?" asked Max.

"Nothing you need concern yourself with," said Isabl.

"You'll have enough to think about at the CMI," added Charl. "Shall we?"

"Yes. Of course," said Ms. Kaplan, who was now gawking at Max like a starstruck fan. "Right this way, Miss

Einstein. It's a forty-minute drive to Jerusalem. Would you like to ride up front or in the back?"

"Up front would be fun," she said. "I mean if Charl and Isabl don't mind. I've never been to Jerusalem before. Actually, I've never been anywhere except New York City and some place that I don't remember much because I was really, really young when I left. I think it was out in the country. I remember smelling trees. Apple trees. And cows."

"How fascinating," said Ms. Kaplan, bustling to the van. "Charl and Isabl, you'll ride in the back."

"I can drive," offered Isabl.

"No, thank you," said Ms. Kaplan. "We're not in that big of a rush. We don't need to be at the CMI until dinner."

Max practically leaped into the front passenger seat. She had a wide, picture window view of everything as they drove from the airport into the historic and holy city of Jerusalem.

The van traveled past the glittering Dome of the Rock and the Citadel, which Charl called "The Tower of David." Max wished she had a camera so she could take a selfie with Mount Zion in the background. Max had never taken a selfie before. Then, again, she'd never traveled halfway across the world to the Middle East before, either. She figured there was a first time for everything.

Holy cities don't get much holier than this one.

"Traffic is thick," sighed Ms. Kaplan. The van came to a complete stop. The highway was a parking lot.

"That sign says Begin South," said Max, reading a highway placard. "Do we need to start going south?"

Charl and Isabl both laughed. "The highway is named after Menachem Begin," said Isabl, pronouncing "begin" as "bay-gen."

"He was a former Prime Minister of Israel," added Charl.

"Oh," said Max, who was always happy to learn new things. Her mind was like a sponge—always looking for information to soak up.

Eventually, after crawling through the rush hour traffic, they arrived at the CMI's headquarters, which turned out to be a nondescript, all-glass modern building. Its mirrored walls helped it blend in with all the buildings surrounding it.

"The benefactor insists that we keep an extremely low profile," explained Ms. Kaplan as she tapped a security code on a pad next to the main double doors. There was a very discreet "CMI" etched into their frosted glass. "Your room will be in the dormitory, just down the hall from the others."

"Are they students like me?" asked Max.

"For the most part," answered Ms. Kaplan. "A few have

already graduated college. But you should get along just fine. You're all very close in age."

"Even the college graduates?"

"Actually, those two might be a little younger than you. One is eleven. The other twelve."

"I'm twelve, too," mumbled Max. "Didn't get to finish college…not yet, anyway."

"Don't let it worry you," said Charl.

"You're every bit as bright as the other contestants," added Isabl.

"Contestants?" said Max. "You guys didn't say anything about 'contestants.' Is that something else that will be explained 'later'?"

"No," said Charl, somewhat mischievously. "The contest will be explained *now*."

21

Ms. Kaplan led the way into a large and noisy dining hall.

Max immediately felt awkward. She was supposed to spend days with kids her own age? She counted eight of them seated around one large, circular table. They were passing around serving platters and bowls heaped with steaming food. There was one empty seat at the table.

Max turned to Charl and Isabl. "Who are these guys?" she whispered.

Isabl smiled. "Your competition."

Max realized Charl and Isabl had left that part out of their invitation to Jerusalem and the CMI. The competition part. They'd left out the other kids part, too.

"Most of the children arrived yesterday," said Ms. Kaplan. "A few the day before…"

"A robot could make better kielbasa than this!" shouted one boy with what sounded like an Eastern European accent. He had just taken a bite out of the sausage speared on his fork. "Robots would produce a much more consistent blend of meats packed into the casing."

"I don't eat anything with a face," said a Japanese girl with long, straight hair seated directly across the table from the boy. "Plant-based nutrition has been scientifically proven to be much healthier for you. It's also healthier for the environment. It takes fifteen pounds of grain to produce one pound of beef. What a waste of water."

"Robotic irrigation could do it much more efficiently—"

"They'd need to tap into the proper aquifers to lessen the environmental impact," added a freckled girl with a lilting Irish accent.

"And they would!" said the sausage boy. "They're robots!"

"Here you are, Max," said Ms. Kaplan, handing Max a clear name badge with a shiny microchip embedded inside its plastic. "Go take a seat with the others."

The empty seat at the table was for Max.

She shyly sat down.

"Who are you?" asked the boy to her right. His name tag ID'ed him as Keeto.

"Max," she mumbled.

"You from America?"

Max nodded.

"Me, too. Oakland."

"New York."

"Weird."

"I beg your pardon?"

"I think it's weird that they thought they needed two Americans in this competition. Everybody else is from other countries…"

"So, um, do you know anything about this contest?"

"Yeah," blurted the blond boy across from Max, the one with half a sausage speared on his fork, the other half in his mouth. "He knows that I'm going to win it!"

"In your dreams, Klaus!" shouted Keeto.

"Those two are like that," whispered a girl seated to her right. She sounded like she might be from Africa. She leaned closer to Max and her dark puffy hair brushed against Max's wild curls. "They're so competitive. Just ignore them. I'm Tisa. From Kenya."

Max nodded, smiled, and decided to eat the rest of her meal in silence.

When dessert (platters of cookies, bowls of fruit, and ice cream drizzled with chocolate sauce, Max's favorite) was finished and the table had been cleared, Ms. Kaplan stepped forward to address the group of nine.

"Good evening to you all. Welcome to the Change Makers Institute. By now, you are probably all wondering why you are here."

"To eat delicious if somewhat imperfect food," said the sausage boy.

"We're glad you enjoyed your meal, Klaus," said Charl. "But this is about much more than food."

"Indeed," said Ms. Kaplan, clasping her hands behind her back. A three-dimensional holographic video screen hovered over the circular table. It started to illustrate the key topics in Ms. Kaplan's speech.

"Food and water security. Economic inequality. Global warming. The education crisis. Poverty. Large scale conflicts and war. Pandemic disease."

"The world you children will soon inherit from your parents is plagued by a plethora of problems," said Ms. Kaplan. "Many of them could threaten the extinction of the human race. Many of them were, of course, created by humans."

"Thanks, Mom and Dad," muttered a dark-eyed boy named Vihaan. *Whoever they might be,* thought Max.

"Here at the CMI, we hope to help reverse this spiral of doom," Ms. Kaplan continued, the graphics in the translucent video dome changing from images of impending

99

disasters to the CMI's sleek, rotating logo. "We aim to make significant changes to save this planet and the humans who inhabit it. That is why we will be sponsoring one brilliant child to help solve Earth's very real problems. One of you. The best and brightest children that your generation has to offer. Each of you has been invited here because of your unique talents, incredible intellects, and, perhaps most important, your humanity."

Max had long dreamed that, one day, she might get a chance to make the world a better place.

Sure, it was probably an impossible dream given her circumstances.

But she believed in what her hero, Dr. Einstein, had once said: "Only a life lived for others is a life worthwhile."

Of course, the good doctor forgot to mention the part where, to do the most good, you had to first *outdo* some very heavy competition.

Eight of the smartest, most gifted, most talented kids on the planet.

22

"You have all been chosen for this competition by the CMI's extremely wealthy benefactor. This person is financing everything—your travel, your food and lodging, your continued education—because our benefactor firmly believes that one of you nine will ultimately be the key to saving Earth."

"If I may," said the girl who only ate plants, "who is this munificent benefactor?"

"Whoa," said Klaus, the sausage loving boy. "Is this a vocabulary quiz? Because I know what munificent means, too. The same thing as charitable, magnanimous, and unstinting."

Ms. Kaplan did her best to ignore Klaus. "Our generous benefactor prefers to remain anonymous at this time. But when the competition is over and one of you emerges victorious, I feel confident they will want to step out of the shadows to congratulate you."

"Let's cut to the chase," said Klaus, who seemed super competitive. "It's going to be me. So, save yourself some time. Go give this mysterious moneybags a call. Tell him to hop on his private jet, fly over here, and congratulate me."

Ms. Kaplan looked like she'd finally had enough of the sausage boy's interruptions. "If you emerge victorious, Klaus, perhaps we will do as you suggest. However, the contest doesn't officially start until tomorrow, when you all will undergo a series of strenuous examinations."

"Tests?" said Max. "Like in school?"

Max hated tests. She hated the whole rigid structure of school.

"Yes, Max. And, I promise you, these exams will be much more difficult than anything you have ever encountered in a classroom. Even for those of you who have college degrees. After the tests, you will also go through a series of interviews, including one with our resident psychiatrist."

"A shrink?" blurted Klaus. "What for?"

"If you are to be the chosen one, the one protecting humanity's future, then we must be confident that you have the emotional stability required to do the job."

"Right," joked Keeto. "No pressure. Just save the world. Piece of cake."

"These are the rules of the game," said Charl, addressing the group. "If you don't feel you are up to the challenge, you may, of course, leave right now. No hard feelings. Major disappointment, of course, but, as I said, our feelings will not be hurt. In fact, the benefactor anticipated that one or more of you might not want to pursue this incredible opportunity. Should you choose to leave, the benefactor has already arranged for your transportation home."

Home.

Max really didn't have one of those. She also didn't think she'd find one here at the CMI. She was always honest with herself and she could tell, almost instantly, that she didn't have what these other eight kids seemed to have. They all looked so confident. So smart. So accomplished. So used to beating tests and being called the best and the brightest.

"Um, you know what?" said Max, standing up from the table. "Maybe I should leave."

She practically bolted out of the dining hall.

"Max?" Isabl called after her.

"I'm just going to, you know, find the bathroom…"

She hit the hall and dashed up the curved corridor of what was, apparently, a circular building.

I hate tests, she thought. *I don't like competition. Or being judged.*

A quote she read online ran through her head: *"Everybody*

is a genius. But if you judge a fish by its ability to climb a tree, it will live its whole life believing that it is stupid." It turned out the quote was *not* by Albert Einstein—you can't trust everything you read on the internet. But Max still liked the quote anyway.

Max shivered a little. She had to get out of there. Yes, it smelled better than the stables, but she didn't want to be graded on her fishlike ability to climb a tree. She didn't want to spend her life thinking she was stupid. She didn't know how to act around other kids. What if they wanted to talk about music or dancing, or worst of all, boys? She just needed to find where Charl and Isabl had stowed her suitcase and ask them to send her back to America. Maybe someplace other than New York. Maybe San Francisco. San Francisco would be nice. It would also be far enough away that the crazy Dr. Zimm couldn't find her.

She was thinking all sorts of stuff so intently, she practically ran into Isabl, who was suddenly standing in front of her. Proving, of course, that the building was circular, and that Isabl had gone around the other way.

"Hello, Max."

"Hey."

"Thinking?"

"Yes, ma'am. It's sort of what I do best."

"Then think about this. *The world is more threatened by*

those who tolerate evil or support it than by the evildoers themselves."

Max couldn't help but grin. "Now *you're* quoting Albert Einstein."

"Indeed I am. Because I don't want the CMI to lose you. In my opinion, you, Max Einstein, are our last best hope."

"What about all those other kids?"

"They are smart, talented, and extremely intelligent. But Max?"

"Yes?"

"They are not *you*. None of them has ever squatted above a horse stable with other homeless people."

"And that's important, because…?"

"Because, despite your astounding intellect, you never once saw yourself as somehow better than others. You saw those people squatting in the stables as your family because you first saw them as humans. If we are to help save the human race, we must first recognize the humanity in all, no matter their station in life. Now then, shall we return to the dining hall?"

Max sighed. Then she nodded.

"Yeah. Let's do this thing. Let's go make Dr. Einstein proud."

23

"**And now,**" **said Charl, when Max was back in the** room and seated at the circular table, "it is time for you all to meet your competition."

The girl who only ate plants raised her hand.

"Yes, Hana?" said Charl.

"We have already met one another. Well, except for the new girl." She gestured at Max. "The one who almost quit. Your name is Max?"

"It's a nickname, short for Maxine," Max explained.

"Interesting."

"You know one another's names," said Isabl. "Now it is time to know more. To learn one another's strengths and abilities so you can see what you're up against."

Max already had a pretty good idea what she was up

against. Some of these kids had already graduated college. She wouldn't be surprised if a few had their PhDs. But she'd made her choice. She wasn't going to run away from the fight.

"As a reminder," said Ms. Kaplan, "for your continued safety and security, here at the CMI, we only use first names."

Ms. Kaplan pointed a remote at the 3-D screen. "Now then, in no particular order, here are our contestants."

A rotating image of a girl with lots of freckles and fiery red hair hovered over the table. It was annotated with scrolling statistics such as hometown, age, grade point average, awards, hobbies, and athletic activities.

"Siobhan," narrated Ms. Kaplan, pronouncing the name *Sha-von*. "Home country: Ireland. An expert in geoscience. She views the earth as a patient whose maladies can be diagnosed through scientific examination, and, eventually, cured. She hopes, one day, to be able to predict major events such as earthquakes, hurricanes, and floods."

Max was impressed. And Siobhan was only the first contestant.

"Toma," said Ms. Kaplan as the rotating image and stats changed to the brown-haired boy seated on the other side of Siobhan. He was wearing a t-shirt that said GRAVITY IS SUCH A DOWNER. "Home country: China. Toma is a budding astrophysicist, obsessed with the nature of celestial bodies and how this study might lead to an understanding of black holes, dark matter, and wormholes."

"I'm also interested in time travel as well as the origins of the universe," added Toma. "They're kind of my hobby."

Max could relate. They were kind of her hobbies, too.

"Moving on," said Ms. Kaplan. "Hana. Home country: Japan. She specializes in botany, the science of plant life…"

Which is all she ever eats, thought Max with a slight grin.

"Hana has a keen interest in plant breeding—bringing new, sustainable foods to the world table while taking a broad view of the global ecosystem. Next up is Vihaan, from Mumbai."

A boy wearing a kurta, a loose collarless shirt, smiled and waved to the group.

"He has his university degree in quantum mechanics. He hopes to, one day, develop a unified theory of everything, which will explain all physical aspects of the universe."

The next image projected was the pale-skinned sausage lover.

"Klaus," said Ms. Kaplan.

And, as if on cue, the boy belched.

"Home country: Poland. He is an expert in robotics, which, of course, combines many fields of study: electrical engineering, mechanical engineering, and computer science."

"And artificial intelligence," said Klaus. "You forgot to mention artificial intelligence, which is what all of you have compared to me: fake smarts."

Ms. Kaplan ignored him and clicked on to the next contestant.

"Tisa."

It was the girl seated beside Max.

"A biochemist from Kenya. By studying how chemistry relates to biological components, such as cells, Tisa can tell you how living beings operate and, for that matter, how they came into existence."

Max wondered if maybe Tisa might be able to use her biochemical smarts to help her figure out how she, Max Einstein, the girl with a mysterious and unknown past, came into existence.

"Tisa would also like you all to know that, even though her father is one of the wealthiest industrialists in all of Africa, that had absolutely nothing to do with her being selected for this program."

Tisa nodded. "Just sayin'…"

Ms. Kaplan tapped her remote. The image shifted to a girl with very short, dark-blond hair.

"Annika. Home country: Germany. She is a master of

formal logic, which, she would argue, is a type of science, even though it is not based on observations, empirical evidence, or data."

Klaus snorted his disagreement.

"Do you dispute the human advances brought to light by Aristotle and his syllogisms?" said Annika.

"Let's save the debates for later," said Charl. "Ms. Kaplan, please continue. Introduce our two American contestants."

"First, we have Keeto from Oakland, California—a city not far from Silicon Valley. Keeto is a computer scientist who envisions changing the world through algorithms and computer code."

"Count on it," said Keeto, who was kind of cocky. Not as bad as Klaus, but close. "In fact, I plan on becoming the first African-American Steve Jobs or Bill Gates. Maybe both."

"Finally, we have Maxine."

"Just Max, please."

"Very well. Max. She is our most recent arrival and, therefore, we have not had time to load her biographical data into our presentation software. Suffice it to say, she, like all of you, deserves to be here."

"Of course she does," said Klaus as the hologram projector went dark. "In fact, you all belong here. Why? So I have somebody to defeat!"

24

Dr. Zimm was not looking forward to the meeting at the Corp's top-secret headquarters hidden in the mountains of West Virginia.

He had been summoned to the underground bunker by the board of directors. Every man and woman seated at the long, impressively carved table would be a billionaire and the type of person who never tolerated (or forgave) mistakes, glitches, or errors.

They would demand answers.

And, right now, Dr. Zimm didn't have any. He had no idea where Max Einstein could've fled with Charl and Isabl.

Only one thing was certain: she wasn't in Milwaukee. Dr. Zimm had been duped by that shiftless vagrant, Mr.

Kennedy. When he sent Jimenez and Murphy back to deal with the deceitful homeless people at the stables, they were all gone. Vanished. Dr. Zimm suspected someone at the CMI knew of his movements.

But he couldn't tell the board of directors his suspicions. If he did, they would relocate *him* to one of their remote re-education facilities. Probably the one in Siberia.

"You lost her?" asked the Chairman. "Again?"

"I'm afraid so," said Dr. Zimm, standing in front of the panel of seven inquisitors, his hands firmly clasped behind his back.

"What is this, Dr. Zimm? The second or third time?"

"The second, sir. And, I promise, it will also be the last."

"You never should've let her escape in the first place!" said the Chinese member of the board. "She was far too valuable."

"She is the only asset remaining from our original investment," said a stick-thin woman with a German accent. Dr. Zimm knew she controlled one of the most profitable biotech companies in the world. She'd also been very instrumental in initiating the Corp's Einstein Project.

"We need her in Africa!" shouted the mining mogul from China. "We are making so much money from cobalt, we need to diversify our holdings. Branch out. You promised she could deliver the supercomputer we discussed, provided she had sufficient funding. Well, doctor, the funding is there. Where is the girl?"

The Chairman banged his gavel. "Enough. As you might surmise, Dr. Zimm, we are not pleased with your performance."

Dr. Zimm grinned. "And yet," he said, boldly, because he knew he could, "you are stuck with me. I am the only one Max will eventually come to trust. Without me, you will never control her."

"Well, dang," said a white-haired man with a Texas twang, "maybe we don't need her no more. What about that boy your team scouted out for us over there in Poland? Klaus something-or-other. Or that other feller, Vihaan. They're both geniuses like this Max Einstein y'all love so much. We could put either one of them on the supercomputer project down in Africa…"

"Impossible," said Dr. Zimm. "You cannot compare Klaus Kowalczyk or Vihaan Banerjee to Maxine Einstein. Neither one of them are anything like her. They are fundamentally different. Besides. Klaus and Vihaan have also disappeared from our radar."

"You lost them, too?" said the Chairman.

"No," Dr. Zimm said with a defiant smirk. "I did not lose them because I was never following them. But, ladies and gentlemen, their disappearances have led me to a theory as to what might've happened to Max Einstein."

"Based on what?"

"The involvement of Charl and Isabl, our friends at the CMI. They orchestrated the disappearance of Miss Einstein. They might also be the ones responsible for Klaus's sudden departure from Poland and Vihaan's disappearance from India. Several other highly intelligent children have simultaneously dropped out of sight. None of them, however, possess what I would call Miss Einstein's 'unique gift.'"

"What are the CMI's plans?" asked the Chairman.

"I suspect something hopelessly naive and lofty. Something with no profit motive whatsoever. Something noble and grand that will never earn them a penny."

The board chuckled.

They knew greed was the primary force in the universe. Anyone who thought otherwise was worse than a dreamer. They were fools.

"But do not despair," said Dr. Zimm. "I have initiated contact with someone who may provide information that will lead us to Miss Einstein while simultaneously sabotaging whatever plans the CMI might be making."

The Chairman arched his bushy eyebrow. "They *may* provide information?"

"Yes, if the price is right. We are still in the early stages of our negotiation. But *they* reached out to *me*."

"Give them whatever fee they require," said the Chairman. "Then give us Maxine Einstein."

"Oh, I will, sir. I will."

25

The next day began bright and early for Max and the eight other contestants.

After a quick breakfast—featuring healthful food from all over the world—they were sent into a room filled with "testing carrels." Each competitor was assigned their own boxy cube and given several number 2 soft lead pencils. They also received an answer sheet with one hundred rows of dots labeled a, b, c, d, and e.

"Kindly proceed to your assigned cubicle," said the proctor, a stern-looking Israeli woman.

Max had testing cubicle C. Tisa, the biochemist from Kenya, would be next to her in D.

"Good luck, Max," said Tisa with a bright and friendly smile.

"Thanks. I think I'm going to need it."

"Me, too. I hate tests. Or as I like to call them, the rapid and rigid regurgitation of memorized facts."

Max grinned. "They're also a nightmare."

"Yes," said Tisa. "They're that, too."

"So," said Max, trying to make small talk the way she'd seen other kids do it, "your father is a millionaire?"

Tisa laughed. "He used to be. Now he's a multimillionaire."

"Silence, please," said the proctor. "Kindly enter your cubicles and take your seats. You will have three hours to complete this examination. If you need a break to use the facilities, press the button on your work table and one of my assistants will escort you to the lavatory. Keep your eyes on your own papers at all times…"

Max shook her head in disbelief. *How did they think any of the contestants could look at their neighbor's papers?* They were penned in, separated by six-foot-tall walls like cattle on a freight train.

She looked down at the answer sheet, which reminded her of the time she took the SAT test when she was nine years old just to see if she was statistically ready for college. She got a 1580 on the test. The highest score possible was 1600. But Max had thought two of the SAT questions were ridiculous so she didn't bother answering them.

"You may now begin your examination," announced the proctor.

Max used her pencil to slice open the seal on the test booklet.

She skimmed the questions.

Her eyes fixated on the pattern of dots emerging on the answer sheet.

They reminded her of three-dimensional binary super-lattices of magnetic nanocrystals and semiconductor quantum dots, a subject she wished she could learn more about. It would be far more interesting than spitting back facts that everybody already knew.

She daydreamed about quantum mechanics for a full hour. Then her mind drifted off on another sunbeam when the clouds outside the cubicle room's mirrored windows parted.

When the proctor announced, "Five minutes remaining on this portion of your examination," Max scribbled an Einstein quote across the empty rows of circles filling the bottom half of her answer sheet:

The only source of knowledge is experience.

Then she added a quote of her own: "I am not a fish climbing a tree."

After the exam and a light lunch, Max was taken to a room for her interview.

The man asking the questions looked even more serious than the lady who'd been supervising the three-hour written test. He launched into a barrage of questions about Max's hero, Albert Einstein.

Max didn't answer any of them.

Not a single one.

Because all of the questions were about what Einstein did or said or theorized and not enough about *who he was*.

Finally, the exasperated inquisitor asked the one question that Max felt like answering.

"Which of Einstein's concepts would you say has the biggest practical impact on your everyday life?"

"That imagination is more important than knowledge," said Max, giving the words just enough edge to let her questioner know that she thought the whole interview had been exactly like the earlier exam—a ridiculous waste of her time.

That's when Charl and Isabl stepped into the room.

Neither one looked very happy.

"Imagination is more important than knowledge?" said Charl. "Is that why you displayed so little knowledge on your written test *and* here in your interview?"

"Are you failing on purpose, Maxine?" asked Isabl. "Are you really that eager to be sent back to America?"

26

"We had such high hopes for you," said Charl, shaking his head.

He and Isabl escorted Max down the sterile hallway.

"I didn't mean to be rude to the interviewer," said Max. "Honest. I'm sure he's a very nice man. But he kept asking all the wrong questions."

"Is that so?" said Isabl. She and Charl were moving so briskly, Max had to speed walk to keep up with them. "Dr. Einstein is your hero, correct?"

Max nodded. "I'm his number one fan."

"Well, since you didn't like our professional interviewer's line of questioning, what question would you have liked to answer?" said Charl. "Something more open-ended? Maybe, 'Which do you think is the most important of Einstein's theories?'"

"You're kidding, right?" said Max. "You guys know Einstein. You know that's not a very good question."

"How so?"

"Determining the most important of Einstein's theories depends on what's important to you. It's all relative."

Charl actually smiled. It was a tiny one, but Max could tell he was actually amused by her answer.

Isabl halted her march up the corridor so she could whip around and peer into Max's eyes. "What *would* be a good question, then?"

Max pondered her answer. She thought about Albert Einstein's Civil Rights activism. His pacifism, even though his theories were used to help develop the atomic bomb that ended World War II. His constant championing of the underdog.

She had her answer.

"If I were running the interviews for the CMI," said Max, "I would ask each and every candidate one simple question: 'What can people living today learn from Professor Albert Einstein?'"

"And how would you answer your own question?"

"Easy. 'Dr. Einstein can teach us all how to be human.' Wasn't that what you were talking about yesterday, Isabl? When you convinced me not to quit, you said, and I quote, 'If we are to help save the human race, we must first recognize the humanity in all, no matter their station in life.'"

Charl and Isabl looked at each other. Now they were both smiling.

"And what would be the 'human' thing to do right now?" asked Isabl.

"Easy," said Max. "You have all these super-smart kids cooped up in dormitories and testing rooms. You have them spitting back facts and penciling in dots on answer sheets when they all could be learning something new. Have any of them even had a chance to do something fun like, I don't know, take a tour of Jerusalem?"

"You raise a good point, Max," said Charl. "Admittedly, the testing has taken priority over the fun."

"Well," said Max, "you know what Dr. Einstein said: Creativity is intelligence having fun. Your eight geniuses might be more creative if you let them go outside and have a little fun."

"Very well," said Isabl. "Round up the others. We shall arrange for a guided tour of the city."

"Woo-hoo!" said Max, pumping her arm. "Field trip!"

She quickly caught herself.

"Sorry. Was that too loud?"

"No," said Charl. "It was...fun."

27

An hour later, Max climbed into a black, smoky-windowed tour bus with the other "contestants": Siobhan, Keeto, Toma, Hana, Vihaan, Klaus, Tisa, and Annika.

"Yahav will be your driver and chaperone for this outing," said Ms. Kaplan, gesturing toward the young man in mirrored sunglasses and a military-style knit sweater behind the wheel. "Yahav is with Shabak, the Israel Security Agency."

Max tried not to grin. *Yahav from Shabak*—say that ten times fast.

"Yahav will be responsible for your safety outside the confines of the Institute," said Ms. Kaplan. "I will not be traveling with you. So listen to his instructions. Obey his commands. And, please—don't make us regret agreeing to let the nine of you go on this 'field trip.'"

"We won't," said Hana, her eyes locked on Klaus.

"Can we swing by Shlomo Falafel?" asked Klaus. "I hear it's the best in Jerusalem."

"Forget food," said Tisa. "Please. Just for two minutes."

"Never!"

"I'd like to visit the Muslim Quarter. It is home to the best souk shopping in the Old City."

"I don't need a new souk!" said Klaus. "I need falafel."

"A souk," explained Tisa, "is an Arab marketplace or bazaar."

Ms. Kaplan sighed and handed Yahav a passenger manifest.

"These are your nine charges," she said. "Good luck."

"First names only?" Yahav remarked after studying the list. "Don't these kids have last names?"

"CMI protocol," remarked Ms. Kaplan. "First names should be all you require."

"Of course." Yahav gave Ms. Kaplan a crisp salute. She slid the side door shut. "Now then," the driver said to his passengers. "Who wants to eat falafel first?"

Klaus raised his hand.

Yahav glanced down at the list of names. "How about you, Max?"

Max raised her hand. "That's me."

"Ah. So it is. Where would you like to go first?"

"How about the Einstein Archives at the Hebrew University of Jerusalem?"

"Excellent suggestion," said Annika. "I know someone who knows someone. I should be able to wrangle us a pass."

"And we can eat nearby," said Hana. "Some place with vegetarian options."

"Falafel *is* vegetarian!" said Klaus.

"Sounds cool to me," said Keeto.

"Let's go!" added Siobhan.

"We'll take the scenic route through the Old City," said Yahav. "I will point out the top tourism spots."

"I want to try Pasta Basta in the Machane Yehuda Market," said Vihaan, in his soft Indian accent. "I am fascinated by the particles in their pink dish."

"What are they?" asked Max.

"Beet and cream fettuccini with goat cheese."

"Gross," said Klaus. "Beets taste like dirt."

The other kids laughed.

Yahav started the engine.

No one was riding "shotgun" up front in the passenger seat.

No one was paying attention to him. They were all too

excited about the Jerusalem that existed beyond the CMI building.

So no one noticed when Yahav quickly thumbed an urgent text message into the phone he kept cradled in his lap.

28

Jerusalem rolled by the van's windows in all its splendor.

Max thought it was beautiful and amazing and historic. She could totally understand why it was one of Albert Einstein's favorite cities, even though he only visited it once, in 1923. At the heart of the Holy Land, Jerusalem was sacred to so many of the world's major religions. The Jews built their first temple here as a home for the Ark of the Covenant. It was also where Christians believed Jesus Christ was crucified and rose from the dead. For Muslims, Jerusalem was the very spot where the Prophet Muhammad ascended to heaven to receive God's word.

While the rest of the group ate lunch at a restaurant called Manou Ba Shouk near Hebrew University (they served falafel, hummus, and kebabs), Max and Annika, the German master of logic, hurried over to the Levy Building on the university's campus in the Givat Ram neighborhood.

"That's where the Albert Einstein Archives are located," said Annika, who loved Einstein almost as much as Max did. Max figured that's how friendships started. You found something you had in common and built from there. She was willing to give it a try.

Annika's father was a professor who knew a professor who knew another professor who knew an archivist at the Hebrew University. Albert Einstein was a founder of the Hebrew University and one of its most loyal supporters.

The kids from the CMI would be able to see several of his eighty thousand papers, artifacts, and treasures stored in the collection—everything from Einstein's 1896 report card to his handwritten manuscript explaining the theory of relativity to what looked like an Einstein action figure.

Max and Annika, who weren't as interested in lunch as everybody else, would see them first.

"This is amazing!" said Max, who was in heaven as she soaked up everything the Archives had to offer. The building reminded her of a much, *much* larger version of her suitcase stuffed with Einstein memorabilia.

"The university has plans to build a new museum to host

129

these Archives in an abandoned planetarium, although the Prime Minister wanted to build a museum in the shape of Einstein's head!" said Annika.

"So his writings would be back inside his brain?"

Annika laughed. "I suppose so. Of course, a lot of this material is now available online, which makes a great deal of logical sense."

"True," said Max. "But it's more fun to see it up close and personal."

"Agreed," said Annika.

They were studying some of Einstein's letters on social issues, such as nuclear disarmament and the Arab–Israeli conflict. In a letter to the editor of a newspaper, Professor Einstein expressed his hope that the conflict between Jews and Arabs could be resolved by a council composed of representatives from both groups.

"His suggestion in this letter to the editor is quite sound," added Annika. "It might even work today."

Annika and Max toured the Archives for more than two hours. Max memorized everything she could, snapping photographs of documents in her mind. It was helpful that Annika spoke German, the language most of Einstein's personal papers were written in. She was an excellent translator.

One letter, written in English, cracked Max up:

Dear Mr. Einstein,

I am a little girl of six. I saw your picture in the paper. I think you ought to have your hair cut. So you can look better.

Cordially yours,
Ann

She stopped laughing when Annika tapped her on the shoulder.

"Max?"

"Yes?"

"Where are the others?"

"What do you mean?"

"We've been here for two hours and thirteen minutes. Surely even Klaus has finished eating lunch by now."

"You're right. Maybe they decided to go someplace else."

"That doesn't make sense," said Annika. "We agreed to meet here."

"Well, the restaurant is only a few blocks away. We can walk back. See if they're still there…"

Annika nodded. "A wise and prudent suggestion."

They thanked the curators of the Einstein Archives.

"We hope to return with our classmates," said Annika. "If not today, then someday soon."

They reached the lobby of the building.

And saw two suspicious men in black suits lurking under the covered breezeway outside.

One was staring at his phone, reading its screen. The other looked like he was waiting for someone to exit the building.

"Do you know the phone number for the CMI?" Max whispered to Annika.

"Yes. I have it programmed into my smartphone."

"Good. We need to call Charl. No, wait. Isabl. She's a much faster driver."

29

Annika speed-dialed Isabl.

"She suggests we stay right where we are," said Annika.

Max took a step forward and looked out at the two men in suits.

Big mistake.

That one step forward put her directly in a blazing shaft of sunlight.

The man eyeballing the doorway nudged the man working with his phone. Then he pointed. Straight at Max.

"Um, staying right here may not be such a good idea," she said. "Come on."

Max led the way back into the building. Annika followed.

They reached the reception desk where they had been granted access to the Archives.

"Excuse me," Max said as politely as she could so she wouldn't sound panicked. "Is there a back door?"

"Why do you ask?"

"Well, uh, we've already seen the front door. We're both visiting Jerusalem for the first time and, um, we want to see as much new and interesting stuff as we can. It's like Dr. Einstein said: 'The important thing is to not stop questioning. Curiosity has its own reason for existing.'"

"So true," said the receptionist. She pointed down a hallway. "Go up this corridor and take a right. You'll be outside on the campus. The Bloomfield Science Museum is just across the lawn. Follow the footpaths. They have a fascinating exhibit about Professor Einstein."

"Thank you!"

Max grabbed Annika by the hand and practically dragged her up the hallway.

Behind them, they could hear heavy footfalls followed by two brusque men speaking roughly to the receptionist.

"Where did those two children go?" said one.

"Tell us. Quick," said the other.

"Have you gentlemen made arrangements to tour the Archives?" the receptionist replied calmly.

"No! We're simply looking for those two missing children."

"Gentlemen, this is an institute of higher learning. The Hebrew University. The only 'children' we allow in here are college freshmen…"

The voices faded. Max was pretty sure the receptionist (who seemed like a pretty tough cookie) would call the police if the two men persisted in barging into the building.

Max and Annika raced out an exit that took them into what looked like a small pocket park—a lawn dotted with shade trees and slender evergreens.

"The museum's over there," said Annika, who had Google-mapped a walking (or running) route to their destination because it was, of course, the logical thing to do. "We should be there in six minutes."

"Five if we run like our lives depend on it," said Max, breathing hard.

"Do they?" panted Annika.

"Yes. I mean, I think so. I'm like ninety-nine percent sure those two men in the black suits are related to some bad guys I met back in New York City."

"Based on?"

"The New York goons were wearing black suits, too."

"That is a logical conclusion, I suppose," said Annika.

"Although it may not be wise to harbor prejudices based on suit colors."

"Trust me on this one, Annika."

"Of course."

Annika picked up her pace and led the way. They were running down a tree-lined cobblestone path that took them to a street.

"There's the museum!" said Max. "Text Isabl. Tell her to meet us there."

"On it."

Annika's thumbs danced across the glass screen on her phone while she jogged up the winding road ahead of Max. Annika was an awesome multi-tasker.

"Isabl texted back," Annika reported. "She'll be here in ten minutes!"

"Good." Max chanced a look over her shoulder.

She didn't like what she saw.

One hundred yards behind them, the two men in black suits were rounding a bend, pointing at the two girls who had foolishly paused to catch their breath on the terrace outside the science museum's main entrance.

"What's inside?" Max asked Annika.

Annika consulted her phone again. "Child-friendly, hands-on exhibitions," she read from her search results.

"So there will be lots of little kids?"

"A logical assumption," said Annika. "Especially near the 'Blue Blocks Station': a large area to 'play, build, and experiment with huge blue blocks in various shapes and sizes.'"

"Let's go," said Max. "If there are a bunch of kids, there'll also be a bunch of parents. The men in the black suits won't dare make a move on us in front of so many witnesses."

And that's how Max and Annika ended up leading a group of museum-going kids in the ten-minute construction of a twisting, spiraling DNA model made entirely out of interlocking giant blue blocks.

30

It was seven a.m. in Boston.

Two p.m. in Jerusalem.

Dr. Zimm stared anxiously at his satellite phone, as if, by staring, he could somehow make it deliver the message he'd been waiting for about Max Einstein's whereabouts. He'd made a deal with an agent who had weaseled his way inside the Change Makers Institute's Israeli headquarters and, for the right price, was willing to betray everything he had sworn to defend.

The undercover informant had confirmed that a young girl named Max was among the nine "child prodigies" undergoing rigorous testing and evaluation inside the CMI building. The girl had shown a keen interest in all things related to the late Albert Einstein.

Of course she had, thought Zimm. *How could she resist, given who she is?*

But why had Charl and Isabl taken the girl to Jerusalem?

And why were they treating Maxine Einstein as if she were just another, run-of-the-mill genius?

Didn't they know who she was? Where she had come from?

Apparently not.

Otherwise, they would have taken much more stringent security precautions. How could they let her go, unguarded, into a public place like the Einstein Archives at Hebrew University? Why hadn't they screened their "security personnel" more carefully?

Because, Dr. Zimm thought with a grin, *they have no idea who they are up against. Me. And the Corp, of course.*

The confirmation that the girl was in Jerusalem had bought Dr. Zimm some time with the Corp's fretful board of directors. Now his two operators—former special forces officers who liked the Corp's salaries better than their country's armed services'—simply had to nab the girl, transport her out of Israel, and deliver her back where she belonged: with Dr. Zimm.

The phone thrummed.

Dr. Zimm snatched it up.

"Yes? Status update, please."

140

"We lost her," said the voice on the other end.

"How?"

"Her friends have friends."

"What?"

"The science museum is swarming with Shabak security officers. I think some of her protectors might also be Mossad."

Mossad. The Israeli national intelligence agency. Their CIA.

"What about Yahav?"

"He is with them. He plays his role well. Came screeching up to the museum in a minibus filled with seven children. Different races. Different nationalities. However, at this moment, the curly-haired girl you're looking for is surrounded by a small army of security guards."

Dr. Zimm considered this new development.

The involvement of Mossad meant that, perhaps, Charl and Isabl *did* have an inkling as to who Max Einstein truly was. It also seemed that the Israel Defense Forces would be guarding her the same way they would protect any extremely valuable human asset.

He reached a decision.

"Stand down," he told his operators. "Head for the border. Israel has too much security. If Yahav has not blown his cover, as I must assume you two have blown yours, he will be able to continue tracking Miss Einstein's movements. If she leaves Jerusalem, we'll have a better chance to grab her—far from the protection of Mossad. We've waited this long, we can wait a little longer. Enjoy your time in Lebanon."

Dr. Zimm disconnected the call.

It was now 7:05 a.m.

He would wait to make his next call. It was too early in the morning.

The news about Max Einstein would make the Chairman of the Corp grumpy enough.

He'd be even grouchier if the call came before his first cup of coffee.

31

Security guards swarmed through the Bloomfield Science Museum.

They formed a human barricade around Max, Annika, and Isabl.

"We're secure," shouted several men and women decked out in what looked like full riot gear: helmets, body armor, and serious weaponry.

"Why did you two wander off from the group like that?" demanded Isabl. She sounded angry.

"We didn't 'wander off,'" said Max. "Annika and I just wanted to skip lunch and visit the Einstein Archives as soon as we could."

"Without your chaperone?" said Isabl. Now she sounded exasperated. "Why do you think we had a Shabak officer driving the minibus? The Shabak is the unseen shield here in Israel. Yahav is a highly skilled security officer."

"Yahav and the others were scheduled to join us at the Archives," said Annika coolly. Her logical mind failed to fathom how she and Max could be at fault in this situation. "Why did it take them two hours to complete their lunch? Falafel is considered *fast* food in most cultures…"

"The other kids voted to go to the bazaar," said Yahav, pushing his way through the phalanx of armed security personnel. The seven other contestants were right behind him.

"Actually," said Keeto, the American from Oakland, "that was mostly your idea, dude."

"Because Tisa had her heart set on visiting the souk," Yahav explained, sounding very defensive, especially for a big, tough security guy.

"I would've been happy to go there after we toured the Einstein Archives," said the girl from Kenya.

"It would've been too crowded," said Yahav. "Too much traffic."

Now he sounded even more defensive.

"This is exactly why we need autonomous automobiles controlled by robots," said Klaus. "There would be no traffic jams with robots…"

While Klaus blathered on about the beauty of driverless

vehicles, Max noticed Isabl subtly arching an eyebrow as she studied Yahav's face. Was she silently questioning her decision to entrust him with the safety of her nine CMI charges? She should be, because Max sure was.

"Natan? Rifka?" Isabl called out to a man and woman on the security team. "I want you two to drive the bus back to the Institute. Yahav?"

"Yes, ma'am?"

"You are relieved of your duties. Please report to your commanding officer. He will advise you of your new assignment."

"But it wasn't my fault," he insisted. "The two girls wandered off."

"With your permission," said Annika.

Max smiled. This was another good thing about having a friend, she realized. They could say the things she wished she'd said.

Isabl turned to Max. "You're riding back with me."

"Yes, ma'am."

The car ride back to CMI was tense. Not because Isabl drove like a maniac. In fact, she didn't. She drove very, very slowly. She also didn't say a word. For five full minutes.

Finally, she spoke.

"You scared us all."

"We were fine," Max told her. "The two men never

really threatened us. Well, they did. Sort of. But we ran away. Don't forget, I'm a city kid. I have street smarts. I know how to handle myself in tough situations."

"Oh, is that so?"

"Annika and I are safe, right? Besides, we got to tour two amazing museums. The Einstein Archives *and* the Bloomfield. The Archives are so awesome. Since Annika's from Germany, she could read all of Dr. Einstein's letters and postcards and she recognized some of the places in the photographs…"

Max babbled about her adventures in the wonderland of Einstein-abilia for the whole ride.

Isabl let her.

By the time they reached the CMI building, they were both smiling and laughing.

It'd been a good day. A little scary, but good.

But that's what life was all about. Taking risks. Facing challenges. And if you did those things with someone, if you survived together, you became friends rather quickly, Max had discovered.

"You need to be more careful, Max," remarked Isabl. "If you try to navigate unknown waters, you run the risk of a shipwreck."

"True," replied Max. "A ship is always safe at the shore. But that's not what it was built for."

"Touché," said Isabl. "You win. But remember, Max—not everybody is interested in changing the world in the same way we want to. Others would prefer to change it in a way that makes them wealthier."

They parked in the garage underneath the CMI building and made their way to the elevator.

"You'll want to make it an early night tonight, Max," Isabl suggested.

"How come?"

"In light of today's incident, we're accelerating the schedule."

"For the contest?"

Isabl nodded. "Tomorrow morning, you will all be taking one more, final exam."

"Another test?"

"Yes. And this one will take eight hours."

32

"This final written exam will help us determine which one of you wins this competition," Ms. Kaplan told the group of nine when they assembled in the dining hall the next morning.

"Will it really take eight hours?" asked Toma.

"Yes," answered Ms. Kaplan. "And you'll probably wish you had eight hours more. I won't sugarcoat this. The questions are extraordinarily difficult. I will be surprised if any of you actually finish the entire test. Do your best. Answer as many questions as you can."

"I wish I'd built a robot to take this test for me," groused Klaus. "A robot could finish it in six hours."

"A quantum computer could finish it even faster," remarked Vihaan, the student of quantum mechanics.

"Yeah," cracked Keeto. "Too bad nobody's invented one of those."

"To build one," offered Max, "you'd have to stretch your mind beyond where Albert Einstein stretched his."

"We're still young," cracked Siobhan. "Maybe one of us will!"

Max smiled. "Maybe."

"Indeed," said Ms. Kaplan. "But before you go off and invent anything, you need to take this test!"

"When I ace it and win the contest," said Klaus, "will there be a party? If so, I'd like to request kielbasa *and* bratwurst."

"We'll keep that in mind, Klaus," said Ms. Kaplan, rolling her eyes. She turned to several CMI staff members. "Proctors? Kindly escort our guests to their testing rooms."

The nine contestants were shuttled off to private testing rooms. They were completely on their own with only the questions, a pen, and a blue answer booklet.

Max looked at the long list of questions. A speed reader, she flew through all fifty in about three minutes. While she was at it, she went ahead and memorized them, too. That would make it easier for her to strategize her attack on the exam.

The questions covered so many topics and required

complex, detailed answers about advanced algebra, very advanced algebra, multi-variable calculus, wave mechanics, quantum physics, and everything in between.

Max knew that Professor Einstein probably would've done very well on this exam, especially the questions about his most famous equation, Energy equals Mass times the speed of Light (C) squared.

She also knew Dr. Einstein hated tests. He called the rigorous exams he was forced to take in high school "a nightmare." In his papers, he argued that pursuing work with intellectual curiosity was a more effective way to learn than to study and memorize things for an exam. He once remarked that it's a miracle that curiosity can survive a formal education.

Max agreed.

She pondered the list of fifty questions.

What would Einstein do? she wondered.

The answer hit her.

She would only answer two of the questions.

The final two: 49 and 50.

Twenty minutes after being sent to her testing room, she turned in her exam booklet.

Ms. Kaplan looked shocked.

"You're already finished?"

"Yes, ma'am. And I want to thank you for the very thorough and difficult test. It was really challenging. So much to think about. Some fascinating areas of inquiry. And, not to brag, but, well—I think I nailed it!"

33

Test completed, Max wanted to go outside and explore the streets and neighborhoods of Jerusalem some more.

"I'd really like to visit Yad Vashem—the World Holocaust Remembrance Center," she told the guard barring the exit out to the street.

"You are to remain inside," said the man, who was wearing wraparound sunglasses even though he was indoors. He was also wearing a bulletproof vest and had a stocky machine gun slung over his shoulder.

"But it's such a lovely day."

"No one leaves the building. Orders from Charl, Isabl, and the benefactor."

"Who, exactly, is this benefactor?"

"The one who is paying for you kids to be here. The one who sponsors everything the Change Makers Institute has done and will do. The one who pays my salary."

"Right. I know that. But who is he?"

"Who said it's a he?" asked the guard.

"Have you met him…or her?"

"No. No one in Jerusalem has."

"Max?" Charl came up the corridor. "You've completed your final exam?"

"Yes, sir."

Charl rocked his wrist and looked at his watch. "You had eight hours."

"I know. But I didn't really need that much time. I was hoping I might do a little more exploring." She gestured toward the door.

"After what happened yesterday? Impossible. The Corp knows your location. You are at risk. So is the CMI and its mission. Kindly return to your room."

"Do as Charl suggests," said a second security guard, stepping out of the Shabak team's small office near the Institute's front doors. It was Yahav. The van driver. Max figured he'd been given desk duty after what happened at the Einstein Archives.

Good, she thought. It's like Tisa had said earlier, "Dude deserves to be demoted."

"You will be summoned to a reading of your results after all the tests have been scored and evaluated," Charl told her. "For now, return to your room. Read. Relax. Stay safe."

Max did as she was told.

In her room, she popped open her battered suitcase and added a new souvenir: a black-and-white postcard of Einstein happily riding a bicycle. She'd purchased it at the Bloomfield Science Museum gift shop—right before Isabl and the security team charged into the building.

Max spent nine long hours looking through her memorabilia, reading, and talking to her inner Einstein, until finally someone rapped on her dorm room door.

"Max?" It was Ms. Kaplan. "It's time. They will see you now."

"They?" asked Max. "Who are they?"

"The council of five."

"Oh-kay. And who are the council of five?"

"The judges. The ones who will help the benefactor decide which of you is the change maker we need. It is a decision that will be finalized within the next twenty-four hours."

Max nodded. Apparently, "the chosen one" was about to be chosen.

34

Ms. Kaplan led Max to a dimly lit room.

Five very serious individuals, all of them dressed in black, sat behind a long table like a panel of stern elders. They were individually illuminated by five overhead spotlights that, shining straight down, turned their faces into craggy collections of harsh shadows.

In the middle of the room, above the judge in the center, glowed a tiny red light inside a gray plastic dome.

Max had a funny feeling that this session was being observed at some remote location via a closed-circuit video camera.

She sensed the benefactor would be judging her, too.

"Welcome, Max," said the wise-looking man in the middle of the panel. His voice was deep and mellow. His goatee beard, tufts of white hair, and wire-rimmed glasses made him look like a kindly professor. Or maybe a wizard. He smiled at Max. Max smiled back. "We five have been chosen to help the benefactor select our instrument of change."

The kindly woman sitting to his right spoke next. "We, of course, have endeavored to give you and the other contestants every opportunity to succeed. For this is a once in a lifetime opportunity. Not only for each of you, but also for our planet."

"If we choose incorrectly," said the man in the middle, "the consequences would be worse than dire. They would be catastrophic."

"Whoever we choose," boomed the woman to his left, "must help guide our planet to its best possible future."

Max nodded. "This has been a totally amazing opportunity. I know I can make the world a better place. So can all the other contestants. They're all great. They're also my new friends. Actually, they're my first friends. Well, I mean among people my own age. Mr. Kennedy was my friend…"

Max realized she was babbling. Her enthusiasm was getting the better of her. Again. She took a deep breath.

"At the end of the day," she told the judges, "I want to be like my hero, Albert Einstein. Maybe that's why I have the same last name even though I know we're not supposed

to use last names here at the Institute. I want to change the world for the better. Dr. Einstein once said, 'The ideals that have lighted my way, and time after time have given me new courage to face life cheerfully, have been Kindness, Beauty, and Truth.' Those are the ideals that I want to light my way, too."

"Well said, Miss Einstein," remarked the man in the middle of the table. "Why then, if you so thoroughly understand the significance of this opportunity, did you fail your written examination so miserably?"

"Why," demanded the woman to his right, consulting her notes, "did you complete it in twenty minutes when you were allotted a full eight hours?"

"Why did you only answer two questions?" added the angry looking judge at the end of the panel. "Were you in a rush to return to your room and watch your favorite YouTube videos?"

"No, sir." She was stunned. "Did I really fail the test?"

"Of course you did!" sputtered the angry judge. "As I stated, you only answered two questions."

Max nodded. "I know. Those were the only two that needed answering. The other forty-eight were simply a prologue leading up to the two questions that I did answer. Number forty-nine—does science make the world safer? And number fifty—if Einstein were still with us, what would he be doing? If one can answer those final two questions, then they have also answered the previous forty-eight."

The panel looked dumbfounded by her response.

"Would you like me to answer the other questions now? I memorized them all..."

"That won't be necessary," said the man in the middle. "Thank you for your time. You will hear from us after we complete our deliberations."

"Thank you."

Max turned around and was ready to exit when an angry voice cried out, "What was question number seventeen, young lady?"

It was the shrunken judge at the far end of the panel.

She turned to face him.

"'If the universe is infinitely expanding, then how can humans' actions be considered significant?' The answer, of course, is simple. All human life is significant and, therefore, should be honored. At least that's what Albert Einstein would be doing if he were still alive. So, you see, the answer to question fifty took care of question seventeen, too."

35

Max walked back to the dormitory wing of the CMI building.

All the other contestants, except Keeto, her fellow American, were hanging out in the commons area, munching on crunchy Israeli junk food: BBQ Bissli wheat twists and peanut buttery Bamba curls, which Max thought looked like brown Cheetos.

They were being entertained by Klaus, who was wearing a curly yarn dust mop on his head.

"Look at me, I'm Max!" He put on a prissy, high-pitched voice. "Oooh. I *love* Professor Einstein! When I grow up, I want to marry his brain!"

Klaus had not seen Max enter the room. But she was standing right behind him.

He pranced in place, flouncing around to make his curly mop top flop. "Dr. Einstein wrote E equals M-C squared just for me! See, it has M and E in it. ME!" Now he giggled like Max had never giggled before in her life.

The other kids stopped laughing at his imitation. Because they saw Max, even if Klaus didn't.

"Um, Klaus?" said Hana. "You might want to knock it off."

"Why?"

"Because," said Max, "it's hysterical!"

She started laughing. Hard.

"That's me. I'm Einstein's number one fangirl! I want to marry his brain!"

She fell to her knees, her body (and curly hair) shaking with laughter.

The rest of the kids started laughing, too.

They'd all been under a lot of stress because of the eight-hour exam. Laughter was a good way to release some of it.

When Max was able to breathe (and talk) again, she told everybody that she'd seen Keeto go into the judges' room when she came out.

"He's the last one," said Toma. "We've all received our test scores."

"I got an 83," said Klaus, sounding more humble than usual. "How'd you do?"

Max shrugged. "I'm not sure. They didn't give me a score. More like an incomplete."

"I got one of those, too," said Vihaan. "I found the section on quantum mechanics to be so fascinating, I spent four hours crafting my response to question thirty-two."

"I skipped that one," said Siobhan.

"Me, too," admitted Max. "But soon, one of us will be chosen. We'll have to start leading the charge for change."

Tisa nodded. "We'll have to start healing the planet."

"Or find a planet B," said Toma, the budding astrophysicist. "But there is no Planet B. Unless, of course, we find a wormhole our spaceship can time travel through."

"Okay," said Tisa, rubbing her hands together. "Let's play a game. 'Saving the Planet.' First challenge. Climate change. How do we change it back? Go!"

Max hung back. She'd never played a game with kids before. Was she supposed to let them win like when she played chess with Mr. Weinstock?

"Simple," said Hana, hooking her long, dark hair behind an ear. "High speed rail! Like we have in Japan. If more countries invested in the technology, there would be significant carbon emissions reductions."

"Indigenous land management!" shouted Siobhan, getting into the spirit of the game. "Nobody's better at protecting rain forests than the people who've lived in them for generations. Let the locals manage their own environments. If we did that, we could eliminate more than six gigatons of CO_2 from the atmosphere."

"How about improved rice production?" suggested Tisa. "If we could get rice farmers to do things slightly differently, we can dramatically reduce the amount of methane produced by current agricultural techniques."

"Wind turbines!" shouted Vihaan.

"Educating girls, all over the world," said Annika.

"A plant-rich diet!" shouted Hana, the botanist.

"You already said high speed rail," groused Klaus.

"So?"

"You can't have two solutions!"

"Actually," said the ever-logical Annika, "I would hazard to guess that none of the world's problems will ever be resolved with one single solution, Klaus. It will take an amalgam of many."

"Annika's right," said Tisa. "Whoever wins this contest will need all the help and ideas they can get."

"They'll need intellectual curiosity and imagination," said Max, finally joining in. "Remember what Einstein said: 'Imagination is more important than knowledge.'"

"Oooh," cooed Klaus, putting on his high-pitched voice

and curly wig again. "Einstein said it! He's such a genius. I looooove Albert Einstein."

Everybody in the room cracked up again.

But Max was the one laughing the loudest.

High speed rail = reduced carbon emissions

EDUCATE GIRLS!

Better food for livestock = less methane

↑ Trees = ↓ CO^2

36

Around ten p.m., as the group was discussing their ideas for eradicating poverty around the world, Isabl came into the commons room.

Yahav, the Shabak security officer, was with her.

"The judges will consult with the benefactor and announce their decision tomorrow morning. Before breakfast."

"Good," said Keeto, who'd rejoined the other contestants after learning that he had scored a 77 on his written examination. "If it was after breakfast, I'd be too nervous to eat. And I'm already hungry. That kibbutz-style breakfast buffet you guys have here is amazing! Salad *and* waffles? Incredible and kosher."

"Will the test scores be the only determining factor?" asked Annika.

"No," said Isabl. "They will also consider your first test, your interviews, and all observed behavior."

Great, thought Max.

She'd totally tanked on her first exam.

She'd more or less blown off her interview.

And she'd been observed straying from the herd and being chased out of the Einstein Archives by evil minions working for the Corp.

She didn't have a snowball's chance in a microwave oven of being the "chosen one."

Still, her brief time at the Change Makers Institute had been some of the happiest days of her life.

She was with kindred spirits. She'd actually made friends. With kids her own age. Her intellect had been challenged on a regular basis. She'd seen an exotic foreign land. She'd spent time looking at Albert Einstein's actual writings. She'd eaten strange snack food items.

She'd even enjoyed the rush of adrenaline that came with escaping the Corp thugs with her new friend Annika.

"Will the chosen one operate out of Jerusalem?" asked Klaus. "Or will I get to go home to Poland?"

"You, or whoever is selected, will be immediately sent

out into the field," said Isabl. "Exactly where you might go is TBD, depending on the mission. But the winner can't stay here. We must assume the Corp knows about our operational base in Israel."

"What, exactly, is the Corp?" asked Tisa.

"The bad guys," said Annika.

"They are," explained Isabl, "the exact opposite of the CMI. They are against any and all changes we might want to see in this world."

"Why?" asked Toma.

"Well, if I might quote Albert Einstein—"

"Nope," joked Klaus. "That's Max's job."

Isabl grinned.

"It's okay," said Max. "You can quote him, too."

"And so I shall. 'Fear or stupidity has always been the basis of most human actions.' And to that I must add greed. The Corp isn't stupid. But they prey on fear so they can feed their greed."

The room was silent as everyone thought about what Isabl just said.

"Get some rest," said Isabl. "Tomorrow will prove to be a very exciting and important day. Especially for one of you."

The group broke up and retired to their rooms.

Max was too nervous to sleep. So, lying in her bed, she had another conversation with Albert Einstein. The imaginary one who lived inside her head.

"Your archives were amazing," she thought. "Eighty thousand items. All those documents. I need to start writing things down like you did."

"It is one way to outwit the constraints imposed by time," replied her internal Einstein.

"I'm not going to win this competition," she admitted with a sigh. "I have to face that reality…"

"Ah, but reality is only an illusion, albeit a very persistent one."

"So, what *can* the world learn from you today? What one thing would you have told the judges?"

There was a pause.

As if the imaginary Einstein in her brain was considering his answer.

Finally, it came:

"I would have told them that peace cannot be kept by force. It can only be achieved by understanding."

"Yeah. That's a good one."

"Danke."

"You're welcome."

"And Max?"

"Yes, sir?"

"Your hair does not look as preposterous as that dust mop wig Klaus was wearing."

"Yes, sir. It does. That's *my* reality. And it's pretty persistent."

She stared up at the ceiling.

"I don't want to win this contest. But I don't want to lose it, either. I also don't want to endanger the CMI. Of course, I wouldn't mind outfoxing the Corp again. It was sort of fun. There're so many pluses and minuses to this whole thing. It's enough to make my head spin."

"Remember the bicycle, Max. How do you keep your balance?"

"By moving forward. And not panicking."

"Ah! Exactly. Sweet dreams, Max."

37

"Are you on a secure line?"

"Yes, Dr. Zimm."

"Report."

"The girl will be leaving Jerusalem. Soon."

"Even if she wins this so-called contest?"

"She won't, believe me. But if, by some miracle, she did, she would go on a field assignment for the do-gooders."

"Excellent. The field is much more conducive to a snatch and grab operation. Israel has too many security forces."

"True. However, none of them pay half as well as you and your friends."

"I am glad you are pleased with our arrangement. Keep me posted. When the girl moves, we move. I'd like you to spearhead the operation."

"Of course. I am happy to do so. Provided you keep wiring the funds to my offshore bank account."

"Don't worry. We believe in greed. We will happily feed yours. One more thing."

"Yes?"

"Charl and Isabl. If the opportunity presents itself, kindly remove them from the equation. We'd happily relocate them to one of our holding facilities."

"Consider it done, Dr. Zimm."

"Thank you, Yahav."

38

The next morning the nine contestants were invited to the Institute's main auditorium.

Five stools with seatbacks were lined up in front of a deep-blue velvet curtain. A familiar slogan scrolled across the top of the stage's proscenium arch:

> Never doubt that a small group of thoughtful,
> committed citizens can change the world;
> indeed, it's the only thing that ever has.
> —Margaret Mead

"But one of us has to lead that group," mumbled Annika, sounding nervous.

"Indeed," said Tisa. "We have to be the change we wish to see in the world."

"Mahatma Gandhi said that," said Toma and Hana, both trying to say it first. Both still trying to prove that they were the smartest kid in the class.

The nine contestants were seated in the front row of the sea of seats. Max realized that the eight other finalists had always been considered the best and the brightest. She wondered if any of them had ever failed at anything before. Probably not. And yet, today, eight of them would. Okay, maybe just seven. Max had already accepted that she had been quickly eliminated from the competition. Those who scored incompletes on their final exams were seldom promoted to the head of the class.

"You guys are all amazing," Max told the group. "It was an honor to even meet you. And Klaus?"

"Yeah?"

"I hope you build that sausage-making robot one day."

"Thanks. Sorry about the bit with the mop wig."

"No worries. I thought it was fantastic. I think all you guys are fantastic."

"Do you think your pal Dr. Einstein would agree?" asked Keeto, whose nerves had dampened his usual swagger.

"Definitely. He knew kids had all the answers."

"You're going to quote him again, aren't you?" laughed Klaus.

"Totally. 'Do not grow old, no matter how long you live. Never cease to stand like curious children before the Great Mystery into which we were born.'"

"Well," said Siobhan, gesturing toward the stage, "it looks like this morning's Great Mystery is about to be resolved."

The five judges marched onto the stage and took their seats on the stools.

"Do you think all the clothes in their closets are black?" whispered Annika.

"Probably," Max whispered back.

"They're judges," said Tisa. "It's a law."

Charl, Isabl, and Ms. Kaplan entered the auditorium and found seats in the second row, right behind the nine kids.

"Good luck, you guys," said Isabl.

"Thanks," was the unanimous whispered reply.

The lead judge, sitting in the center of the panel again, cleared his throat.

Max knew: It was time for the verdict to be delivered.

Annika reached over and took Max's right hand. Tisa took her left. Max squeezed back tightly. In a chain reaction that would've made Dr. Einstein proud, all nine contestants were soon clutching one another's hands. In a few short days, the nine strangers had, somehow, become a family.

"We have made our recommendation to the benefactor," said the lead judge.

"Although our verdict was not unanimous," grumbled the sour-faced judge who looked even angrier than he had the night before.

The lead judge took over again. "The benefactor advised us that they would be taking several, shall we say, variables and extenuating circumstances into account before arriving at their final selection."

"None of you should feel that you are somehow 'less than' the first finisher," added the most motherly judge. "On the contrary. Just being here means you are special… you're all winners…"

And on and on they went.

Max knew they were trying to be kind. To soften the blow. But their well-intentioned preamble was excruciating. Sooner or later, they'd just have to come out and name the winner. Or the "first finisher" if "winner" wasn't a gentle enough word for the panel to use.

"Cut to the chase, dude," muttered Keeto.

"Totally," echoed Vihaan.

Finally, the judge in the center stood up. He pulled a

sealed envelope out of his suitcoat's interior pocket.

"The Change Makers Institute, in accordance with our benefactor's wishes, is pleased to announce our first finisher."

He sliced open the envelope with his index finger.

It seemed to take an hour for him to complete the task. Another prime example of the theory of relativity at work in everyday life.

The judge read what was on the paper.

Grinned.

Looked straight at Max.

"Congratulations, Max," he said. "You are the chosen one."

39

Max couldn't believe her ears.

She'd won?

Some of the other kids started sobbing. Even Klaus was screwing up his nose, trying not to cry.

"Congratulations, Max," said Annika, struggling against the tears that were filling her blue eyes. "I'm happy for you."

"Me, too," said Tisa.

Happy? They both looked miserable.

Max probably should've felt elated. Maybe she should've jumped up and down and pumped her fists and done some kind of victory dance.

Instead, she felt horrible.

She hated seeing her new friends so down and discouraged, their spirits crushed by what they all probably felt was the biggest defeat in their young lives.

"You guys?" is all she could say. "I'm sorry...I didn't..."

"Max?" said the head judge.

She turned to face the stage. She had to sniffle back her own tears.

"Yes, sir?"

"Please report to the briefing room in two hours to receive your first CMI assignment and meet your team. We've assembled some of the best scientists and engineers in the world to assist you in your task. The rest of you? Please enjoy one last breakfast buffet and then, at your earliest convenience, pack your bags. It is time for you to return home, where, we are certain, you will all continue to do great and amazing things."

Max's eight friends, her former rivals, stood up. Nobody was holding hands. Max missed that. She liked the hand-holding.

"Congratulations, Max," said Charl from the row behind her.

"Once you are properly briefed," added Isabl, "we will be pulling you out of Israel."

"It's too hot here," added Charl. "And I'm not referring to the temperature."

"We need to stay one step ahead of the Corp," said Isabl.

"Indeed, you do," said Ms. Kaplan, giving Max a look of disdain. The CMI matron undoubtedly figured the sudden appearance of the Corp in Jerusalem was all Max's fault, which, come to think of it, it probably was.

Max watched the eight other contestants, their heads hanging down, shuffle out of the auditorium.

They all seemed so sad. Broken. All their spirit and fiery passion had, in the instant of the announcement, been extinguished.

That was a huge problem.

One for Max to solve.

Because that's who she was.

A problem solver.

Just like Albert Einstein.

40

Two hours later, as requested, Max reported to the briefing room.

It was the same room where she'd first met her competition. Once again, the holographic map of the globe was rotating over the circular desk. Red spots glowed and throbbed all over the world. In Africa. The Amazon rain forest. Washington, DC. London.

She figured those were the trouble spots where the CMI was hoping to accomplish some kind of significant change. Charl and Isabl were in the room. So were the head judge and eight strangers Max had never met before.

More strangers, Max thought. Now that she actually had some friends, kids her own age, she was a little wary of starting over with a new group she knew nothing about.

181

"Max?" said Isabl. "Welcome. It's time for you to meet your team."

"My team?"

"Our benefactor handpicked these eight ladies and gentlemen to assist you on your first mission, which you, of course, will help select."

"So, I get to help pick the mission but not the mission team?"

"These scientists and engineers are all tops in their fields, Max," said Charl. "For instance, Dr. Sherpa here is an expert in quantum mechanics."

"So's Vihaan."

"Professor Huang specializes in agricultural issues."

"Is she smarter than Hana?" muttered Max.

"Mr. Okusi is a computer scientist—"

"That's Keeto's department."

"Max?" said Isabl. "You're being difficult."

"Sorry. But sometimes, I just can't help it." She turned to the group of esteemed scientists and engineers. "Um. Hi. Glad you could make it. Hope it wasn't a wasted trip, but, well, it might've been."

She gestured to another one of those smoky ceiling domes shielding what had to be a security camera. "Is our friend watching us?"

"Which friend?" asked Isabl.

"You know—Mr. or Ms. Benefactor."

"I'm not sure."

"I'd like to talk to him or her about my team."

"But these are his rules," added Charl. "This is *his* team."

"Good. We settled that one," said Max. "He's a he."

She shook her head. *Rules. Restrictions. Dictates.* She liked those about as much as Einstein did, which was *not at all.*

She walked up to the camera. "Hello, sir. I'm, uh, Max. Max Einstein. And I can't wait to start changing things for the better. So, uh, thanks for the vote of confidence. I'm eager to get started. Today. Right now. Let's do it! Woo-hoo!"

She gave the camera a mighty arm pump.

All the super-serious scientists in the room were gawking at her, some with their mouths hanging open.

"I'm happy to be your first finisher," she said to the camera. "But. Well. But…"

"There can be no 'buts,'" said the head judge. "If you are unwilling to perform your duties as outlined by the benefactor—"

"Oh, I'm willing, sir. In fact, I'm more than willing. I'm eager. However, I do have one little request. Actually, to be honest, it's not really a request. It's more of a demand."

Max wondered if her headstrong enthusiasm for a wild idea might do her in.

The judge raised his bushy eyebrows. "A demand?"

"Yes, sir. And it's nonnegotiable. We're talking zero wiggle room."

"And what is this 'demand'?"

"Well, no offense to the brilliant scientists here in the room, or to you, wise and munificent benefactor."

This time, she comically bowed at the camera.

The main judge touched a clear earpiece that Max had noticed he was wearing.

"What is your demand?" he said, repeating what someone, probably the benefactor, had just said to him.

"Well, it's pretty simple," said Max, focusing on the camera. "I want the other eight contestants to be my team. Siobhan, Keeto, Toma, Hana, Vihaan, Tisa, Annika, and, yes, even Klaus. They have to be my field crew. I don't mind if some of these adults help us with logistics and office stuff, but the kids you assembled here are absolutely brilliant. That's who I want with me. The best and the brightest."

"But they're children!" blurted Professor Huang.

"Exactly right," said Max. "They have no preconceived notions. No fixed ideas about how things have to be done. Their minds are open. They'll see the world with fresh eyes and attack problems with fresh ideas. And, if you ask me, that's exactly what this tired old world needs. As someone much smarter than me once said, 'A new type of thinking is

essential if mankind is to survive and move toward higher levels.'" Max looked up at the camera again. "So, do we have a deal, sir? I hope we have a deal. I love good deals."

The room was silent.

Now everybody was staring up at the concealed security camera.

Finally, the head judge touched his ear and, a moment later, cleared his throat.

"Yes," he said, repeating what he heard through his earpiece. "You have a deal. The eight other contestants can be your field team."

"Woo-hoo!" said Max, giving the camera another arm pump. "We won't let you down! I promise. Or my name isn't Max Einstein!"

41

The eight genius children were asked to join the girl named Max in the main conference room.

"You can finish packing later," said Ms. Kaplan. "You will all be leaving Jerusalem, but there's been a change of plans. You won't be flying home. You'll be traveling with Max. She's requested your help on her first mission."

Yahav heard all this from his post in the lobby of the CMI building.

Charl and Isabl had taken him off the active security detail after the incident at the Einstein Archives. They'd demoted him to a desk job. His only official task was to sign in visitors (like the prominent professors and engineers who'd arrived that morning) and issue ID badges.

It was the perfect post for him to continue his undercover surveillance work for the Corp.

From his post in the lobby, Yahav knew who was coming into the building and what was going on at all times. And judging from the flurry of activity and the flow of very important guests that day, he could tell that something big was definitely up.

The Institute might soon be making their move with Max Einstein.

Yahav stood up. Looked up and down the corridor. The other little geniuses had just been summoned to the main conference room.

That meant the dormitories were empty.

Perfect, he thought.

He pulled a plastic toy out of the hip pocket of his cargo pants. It was a small, solar-powered, plastic figurine of a rumpled Albert Einstein. When sitting in the sun, the plastic Einstein would continuously tap the side of his crazy-haired head, as if he were having an idea.

On an earlier reconnaissance mission through the CMI dormitory, Yahav had noticed that the girl, Max, kept an assortment of Einstein memorabilia displayed in a battered suitcase that she opened up like a curio cabinet.

Yahav would add one more item to her collection.

He hung a gift tag around the toy professor's neck: "Good Luck! From your friends at CMI!"

He also inserted a tiny tracking device, about the size of a fingernail, into the toy's base.

Now all he had to do was place the Einstein action figure inside the girl's suitcase and the Corp would know where she (well, at least her suitcase) was at all times.

He hurried up the hall, stopping to pick up a case of bottled water from a nearby supply closet. If he was discovered in the dorm area, he could say he was there restocking the rooms with beverages.

But everybody—staff and children—was in the conference center.

No one saw him enter Max's room.

No one saw him place the new Einstein souvenir in the suitcase with all the others.

Now that he had activated the tracking device in the base of the toy, Dr. Zimm and the Corp could definitely see where Max Einstein was, no matter where in the world the CMI sent her.

42

"You're the first finisher, Max," said Annika. "It's only logical that you pick your own project."

"Just make sure it involves robots," said Klaus.

"Why?" said Hana. "Max is supposed to do good for humans, not machines."

"We have several suggestions we'd like to make," said Professor Huang. "After all, that's why I was summoned here from the University of California at Berkeley."

"I flew in from Colorado," added one of the adult engineers. "I have some ideas about water shortages…"

Max did her best to block out all the voices and advice swirling around her in the conference room like a swarm of angry bees. She walked up to the center table and studied the glowing trouble spots on the holographic globe as it slowly rotated on its axis.

"What's going on right here?" she asked, pointing to a throbbing red blotch in Africa.

"That's the Democratic Republic of the Congo," said Tisa, the girl from Kenya.

"We would love to bring electricity to some of the remote villages in that area," said Charl.

"It would do a lot of good," added Isabl.

"The DRC has been 'rebuilding' its power grid as part of the war-torn country's reconstruction since 2003," said another one of the professors in the room. "Only nine percent of Congo's seventy million people have access to electricity."

"Most of that is in the urban areas," said Charl. "Only about one percent of the rural areas have electricity. They're totally off the grid."

"My father is very interested in investing in the Congo," said Tisa. "But if the villages lack electricity, it is very hard for him to convince his board of directors to pour money into them."

"Well," said Max, as she slowly worked through a new idea in her head. "What if…what if we could electrify them without a power grid? What if a village could be energy self-sufficient and the national government didn't have to build power plants or run transmission lines or worry about creating utility companies to manage it all?"

"And what if unicorns could fart rainbows?" said Klaus.

Max ignored him. She was deep in thought. Lack of access to electricity was surely hurting Congolese people. Their health, their education, their money-making potential.

That's why they send their children into those mines, she thought.

She stared at the slowly turning globe, remembering that news story she'd read about kids as young as seven "working in perilous conditions in the Democratic Republic of the Congo," where they mined cobalt that ended up in first-world smartphones, cars, and computers.

The children were being paid one dollar a day to do backbreaking work, she remembered.

And then she remembered something that hadn't mattered much to her when she'd read it the first time:

"They were also helping make a shadowy international business consortium called the Corp very, very, very rich."

The Corp.

The bad guys. The ones who'd come after her, first in New York and then Jerusalem.

Maybe it was time to take the battle to them. Or, at the very least, cut off one of their revenue streams.

"These villages without electricity," she said, "are they anywhere near the cobalt mines?"

Charl and Isabl both nodded.

"Some, yes," said Isabl.

"The ones run by, you know, those other guys?"

"An international mining consortium runs the operation," said Charl. "And, yes, they have very powerful, very well-connected friends."

The way he said it, Max knew Charl meant "the Corp."

"If we can bring low-cost electricity to the rural villages," said Max, "then, maybe, the people would be less dependent on the mining industry. Maybe they could generate income some other way."

"They could," said Tisa. "I will talk to my father. If we bring electricity to a village, I am sure he will bring an investment. He might give us a deadline, though. Father is very focused on results."

"And we'll give them to him," said Max, her runaway enthusiasm growing stronger. "If we can bring a village electricity and new hope, maybe they wouldn't have to tear their families apart and send their children down into the mines to pick through rocks with their bare hands."

"So, what do we do?" wondered Vihaan. "How do we bring electricity somewhere that doesn't even have power lines?"

194

"Maybe we don't need power lines or even power plants," said Max.

"Here we go with the unicorns again," groused Klaus, rolling his eyes.

Max could see the answer so clearly. She could see well-lit homes. Less pollution. New industries. And it all started with Albert Einstein's 1905 theory of the photoelectric effect. (It was the theory that won him the Nobel Prize; not the more famous theory of relativity.) The thought experiment was so vivid in her mind that she didn't realize that everyone in the room was staring at her, waiting for her to actually say something.

"What do *you* want to do, Max?" asked Isabl.

"Hmmm?"

"What's the project?"

"Oh. Right. It's simple, actually. We'll help one village generate electricity utilizing photoelectrons bouncing off a surface. We'll show them how to harness the energy in a beam of sunlight."

"Solar power!" shouted Siobhan.

"Exactly."

43

Charl and Isabl pulled up a file on their laptop and displayed its contents through the holographic projector.

"Max's notion fits nicely with a plea the CMI recently received from a village in the Congo," said Isabl. "It's called Kasombumba and lies between Kolwezi and Lubumbashi near the southern border."

"Can you send me the details?" asked Tisa. "I will forward them to my father."

Max nodded. "Working with African investors would be awesome. We'll set up the electricity. The investors can help the villagers plot a new course, free from the mines."

She moved closer to the 3-D images of the village of Kasombumba. It was a ramshackle collection of buildings. Their roofs were sheets of corrugated aluminum. Laundry was strung out to dry. The people puttered around on motor scooters. Max saw a few spindly poles holding up limp wires but no major signs of electricity.

"Is it a mining town?" she asked.

"Yes," said Isabl, clicking her remote to bring up a montage of images of the village and its nearby mines. "The children don't go to school during the day. They go to work."

"Recently," said Charl, "the only school in Kasombumba burned down. It was late at night..."

Max nodded. "Because the kids all work during the day."

"Exactly. They were using a kerosene lamp to light the classroom. Someone accidentally knocked it over. Everyone escaped but the school and all its books were destroyed."

"They need electricity," said Max. "Solar panels..."

"If I may?" said one of the professors, raising his hand.

"Yes, sir?"

"Well, I've been working with a Non-Governmental Organization called Smart Energy Everywhere, or SEE. I'm sure they would gladly offer you their assistance."

"What about the solar panels?" said Klaus. "Will they gladly offer us those, too? Because solar panels cost a whole lot more than assistance."

The professor smiled. "Yes. That is what I meant to say.

I think they might give us a steep discount on the solar panels."

"Excellent," said Klaus. "We'll hammer out a deal and ship the material down to Africa. We do a quick installation and—BOOM!—job done. We can move on to the next part of the planet that needs saving."

Max bit her tongue. She didn't like Klaus's attitude or the fact that he was, basically, trying to take charge. But to bring solar-powered electricity to the mining village, to make sure their next school didn't burn down when somebody kicked over a kerosene lamp, they would definitely need solar panels. This project was bigger than her. She'd play along. Especially since detail work wasn't her number one skill.

"I'll hang back here and work with the professor while you and the rest of the crew go scope out the situation in the village," volunteered Klaus. "I can handle the logistics for getting the solar panels delivered and catch up with you guys later. I'm good with logistics."

"I'll work with my father," said Tisa. "We will hammer out a concrete plan for a new industry or agribusiness to replace the stranglehold of the mining companies."

"And let us know our deadline," said Max.

"Don't worry. Father will be in charge of that!"

"That seems like an excellent division of labor," said

Annika, because she was super logical that way.

Max turned to Charl and Isabl.

"How soon can we leave?"

"As soon as you children get your shots," said Ms. Kaplan, the Institute's den mother.

Max winced. So did everybody else. "Shots?"

"We have to make sure you are up to date with vaccinations," said Ms. Kaplan. "We also need to inoculate you against yellow fever. And then there's the malaria medicine you'll all need to start taking…"

Ms. Kaplan led the way out of the room.

All the kids except Klaus and Max followed her. Klaus was hanging back, chatting with the professor and the other adult scientists in the room.

"Great idea about that NGO, doc," Max heard him say. "I don't know how our first finisher planned on doing solar power without solar panels, but, whatever…"

Isabl came up and tapped Max on the shoulder. "Have you ever been to a doctor for vaccinations?" she whispered.

"Yes. When I was in foster care."

"Good. You'll need the other shots, though."

"Right."

Max headed for the door.

Klaus blocked her path.

"Great working with you, Max. But you know what?"

"What?"

"One day, probably pretty soon, after the benefactor realizes his blunder, I have a feeling I'll be running the group."

"Is that so?"

"Yeah. This gig is all about logistics. Making deals. That's my wheelhouse. I'm good at it. You? You're more of a head case. Dreaming up big ideas. But big ideas don't turn on the lights."

"Well, Klaus, when that day comes," she said, "I'll be happy to work for you. And, of course, your robots, too."

When she said "robots," she gestured to all the grown-ups in the room.

44

The red blip moved slightly.

Dr. Zimm leaned closer to his computer screen.

The blip blinked.

And then it started progressing slowly and steadily up a street in Jerusalem.

The girl was on the move. The tracker Yahav had planted was working.

A text confirmation soon followed: The CMI team is going on a mission. Word is they are heading to Africa.

Dr. Zimm grinned. Yahav had been an excellent investment. He would send the spy a bonus—just as soon as they had the girl back in Corp custody.

He happily watched the flashing red beacon work its way through the traffic-congested city.

Another text scrolled across the screen: Congo. The Polish boy is yelling into a phone. Organizing a delivery of solar panels. A small village called Kasombumba close to Kolwezi and Lubumbashi. Near the southern border.

Could this get any better? wondered Dr. Zimm.

The southern Congo was where some of the Corp's wealthiest members operated their extremely profitable cobalt mines. Labor was cheap. The high-tech world was hungry for Africa's minerals. The Corp members sold everything they could scrounge out of the ground.

They had so much money pouring in from their mining operations, they were eager to branch out into new endeavors. They wanted to finance the research needed to develop what they called a "quantum computer." Normal binary digital computers store bits of information as either a *1* or a *0*. Quantum computers process information quite differently. They use quantum mechanical phenomena such as superposition and entanglement.

Dr. Zimm didn't have a clue as to what those things were. Biology and genetics were his main areas of expertise.

But he understood the financial windfall that would come to whoever perfected a computer that could process information ten times faster than any computer currently in existence.

The Corp members in Africa insisted that no one could

design such an advanced, quantum-physics-based machine unless they had the mind of an Einstein.

Which Max, of course, did.

And they would pay handsomely for her "services."

The board of directors at headquarters would be delighted with Dr. Zimm's bold initiative, again.

Everything was going to be fine.

Dr. Zimm radioed his two associates.

"We need to be in Africa," he told them. "Bring whatever you think we might need to subdue the girl and any of her protectors."

Jimenez and Murphy needed a few hours to pack their gear.

And their weapons.

Dr. Zimm would plot the precise flight plan for the Corp's private jet (it was one in a fleet of two dozen) just as soon as the girl's red dot landed at its final destination.

From his spy, Dr. Zimm knew that Max Einstein was going to the Democratic Republic of the Congo on some do-gooder mission involving solar power for the softies who worked at the CMI.

Well, Dr. Zimm and his team had a mission, too.

They needed to snatch back the one thing the Corp never should've lost: Max Einstein.

45

Max rode to the airport in a van with Isabl, Charl, and seven of the kids on her team.

Klaus would be staying behind in Jerusalem for a day or two with the "growns" (which is what everybody started calling the grownup professors and scientists helping the CMI field team). Klaus, who was quite a brown noser, would be working on those solar panel shipping logistics. He'd also probably be working overtime to become the growns' favorite.

The only adults traveling to the Congo with Max and her crew were Charl and Isabl.

They were in charge of "intelligence and security." If the CMI field team got into any sort of trouble or jam, Charl and Isabl were charged with extracting them from the unsafe situation as quickly as possible.

And, at least according to the United States State Department, the Democratic Republic of the Congo wasn't exactly safe. "The security situation in parts of the DRC," their alert reported, "remains unstable due to the activities of rebel and other armed groups and ongoing military operations. Sporadic but severe outbreaks of violence targeting civilians continue throughout many provinces. The kidnapping of humanitarian workers for ransom money is on the rise."

Great, thought Max when she read the State Department travel warning. *We're humanitarian workers funded by a mysterious but extremely wealthy benefactor. We might as well go to Africa with "kidnap me now" signs on our backs.*

The van entered a secure section of the airfield and parked alongside a very sleek and stealthy looking aircraft.

"It's the benefactor's private jet," said Charl as everybody tumbled out of the van to grab their duffel bags and gear.

"It looks like a spaceship," said Toma, the budding Chinese astrophysicist.

"Almost," said Isabl. "It currently has a ceiling of about nine miles."

"That's a fifth of the way to what we call 'space,'" said Toma. "Of course, a jet can't fly in space. Jets need oxygen."

"Yeah," said Keeto. "Me, too."

"Board up, folks," said Charl. "It's nearly three thousand miles to Lubumbashi."

"Is there food on the plane?" asked Keeto.

"There are meals ready to eat in the galley."

"MREs?" Keeto wrinkled his nose like he smelled something extremely bad. "Rations? Like they have in the Army?"

"Yes," said Isabl. "At the CMI, we like to put our money into helping people, not helping ourselves to luxury items such as gourmet airplane meals."

"That's the way it should be," said Max. "But maybe next time we could splurge for a couple pizzas? Maybe some Chinese food?"

"Point taken," said Charl.

A CMI cargo crew loaded luggage and trunks filled with scientific gear into the belly of the plane. Max and her team climbed up the steep staircase and found seats in the cabin of the jet. They were comfortable, but nothing fancy.

"The benefactor has designed this plane to be extremely fuel efficient," said Isabl, taking a seat next to Max. Charl strapped in across the aisle. "The less weight there is, the less fuel we need to burn."

"You guys are riding back here?" asked Max.

"That's right."

"So, um, who'll be the pilots?"

Charl grinned. "This plane doesn't need pilots. It's totally autonomous."

"Think driverless car," added Isabl. "Only in the air."

"You're kidding."

They both shook their heads.

"The plane navigates itself utilizing GPS," explained Isabl.

"Which only works," said Max, "because of Einstein's theory of relativity."

"Well," said the fiery Siobhan, seated in the row behind Max, "I certainly hope it's more than a theory! Theories don't keep airplanes up in the air!"

The pilotless plane taxied itself to the runway.

"This is so weird," said Keeto.

"Most scientific leaps of faith always seem weird at first," said Tisa.

"But we're about to leap into the air without a pilot," said Siobhan, who could be pretty edgy (and entertaining) when she was annoyed.

When it was cleared for takeoff, the jet rocketed down the runway and gently lifted up into the air. Max thought the ride felt smoother than the flight from New York to Jerusalem. It was quieter, too.

The door to the cockpit was wide open. Everybody could see the yoke and rudder pedals and throttle and all sorts of sliding levers gliding through their automated moves. It was like watching a super high-tech player piano doing two Beethoven concertos at once.

Charl tugged down on his ball cap and closed his eyes. "Nap time," he said after the plane reached its cruising altitude. "Wake me if the plane asks for any human assistance."

"Same here," said Isabl, pushing the reclining button on her seat.

The jet executed a smooth and flawless banking maneuver.

"This is absolutely amazing," said Annika.

"Who is this benefactor?" wondered Keeto. "Tony Stark?"

"And who is this Tony Stark?" asked Vihaan, who, Max guessed, probably spent most of his days with his nose buried in books about quantum mechanics, not make-believe superheroes.

"You know—Iron Man," said Keeto. "From the comic books. He has tons of money and all sorts of cool gadgets like planes that can fly themselves."

That made Max smile.

Was she working for a real-live Tony Stark now?

Or, maybe, somebody even more awesome?

Because they had Max Einstein flying to Africa in their pilotless private jet.

And that sure beat living in a New York City horse stable above a mountain of manure.

46

The team landed (with no pilot in the cockpit) at the Luano International Airport, just outside Lubumbashi, the second largest city in the Congo.

Max was eager to explore the countryside. To wander off and bump into a gorilla or something.

But she was there on a mission. And they didn't have very much time. Tisa received a text from her father in Nairobi.

"Father says he has lined up several investors who are eager to turn Kasombumba from a mining village into a fair-trade garment center," Tisa reported. "But to do so, they will need sewing machines, which father's money people will happily provide, along with training."

Max understood. "We just have to give them the electrical outlets to plug into."

"Exactly," said Tisa. "And we need to do it within the month or the seed money will move elsewhere."

"Deadlines," said Max.

"I told you," said Tisa. "Father loves them."

And Max wished she was better at meeting them. Organization, time management? That wasn't for daydreamers like her.

Lubumbashi, where the team landed, was the hub for the country's major mining companies—including the ones affiliated with the Corp.

Because the land surrounding Lubumbashi was rich with minerals. Cobalt, copper, tin, radium, uranium, and even diamonds. Copper mining had been going on for more than a thousand years. But, because cobalt was needed to make all the high-tech lithium-ion batteries charging the twenty-first century's gizmos, gadgets, and electric cars, it was fast becoming the region's big new money maker.

Some people want to change the world for the better.

Most just want to make money.

Some, like Tisa's father and his eco-friendly investors, actually wanted to do both!

The reddish, rocky terrain reminded Max of the images she'd seen of Mars.

"I'd love to map all this mineralogy," said Siobhan as their vehicle rumbled along a rutted road.

"Next trip," said Max. "This time, we're all about solar power."

Siobhan nodded. "Next time."

The team finally arrived in Kasombumba, where they were greeted by the villagers who had sent the desperate pleas to the CMI.

"We are completely off the grid," explained a man named Patrick. "What little electricity we do generate is fueled with kerosene and cakes of dried dung."

Max smiled slightly. The idea of burning dung reminded her of the stables and her idea for a green gas mill fueled by horse manure.

"We're going to change all that," said Max. "Soon."

"Very soon," said Tisa, gently reminding Max, once again, of their deadline.

"Solar panels are on their way," said Vihaan.

Patrick's son, Emmanuel, who was maybe a year or two younger than Max, offered to show the CMI kids around the village.

"We all work in the mines," he said. "My whole body aches every day. Others have it worse. Many of the miners are younger than me. We dig tunnels by hand."

"Do you wear masks and gloves?" asked Annika.

"No," answered Emmanuel. "We breathe in the dust. Many have mysterious illnesses."

"Well," said Max, "let's hope bringing electricity into your village will be a first step toward changing all that."

"The second step will be shifting to a new economic model," said Tisa.

Emmanuel smiled. "You mean some other way to make money?"

"Exactly!"

Max and her team set up camp in a small circle of tents on the outskirts of the village.

They spent their first day finalizing plans for the solar panel installation as well as the wiring of five homes. That night, they ate some of the local specialties, including grasshoppers and caterpillars.

"We are so far ahead of you," joked Emmanuel. "Insects are a very cheap and tasty form of protein. Much less expensive than cows. It is, as you say, a new economic model."

Max liked Emmanuel. He was smart. She wasn't crazy about this "new source of protein," though. She preferred peanut butter. (Even though the bugs did taste kind of nutty.)

On the second day, Tisa, the chemist, helped the team set up a small lab in a tent.

"We might need to do some chemistry before we're done here," she said. For Tisa, a day wasn't complete without at least one science experiment.

Grasshopper fries

Caterpillar burger

Nutrition per 100g of
grasshopper:

Protein: 20.6 grams
Fat: 6.1 grams
Carbohydrates: 3.9 grams

Looks like
French fries,
tastes like
chicken!

Charl and Isabl spent *their* first days patrolling the countryside, gathering whatever intelligence they could on the bands of marauding outlaws rumored to be roaming through the region.

On the third day in Kasombumba, Klaus finally arrived with a small convoy of light trucks.

He'd brought his own security detail.

Yahav from Shabak. The Israeli agent Max trusted just about as much as she trusted Klaus.

Which wasn't very much.

47

"Yahav?" said Charl. "What are you doing here?"

Charl and Isabl were in camp to greet the arrival of the supply convoy.

Yahav had an automatic weapon slung over his shoulder.

"This is a dangerous hot spot, sir," said Yahav. "Vehicle thefts, burglaries, armed robberies, kidnapping. No way was the benefactor going to allow young Klaus to come into the Congo unprotected. I volunteered for the detail. I'm not the type who can sit behind a desk all day. It made my butt ache."

Klaus giggled when Yahav said the word "butt."

Of course, thought Max.

"Where are the solar panels?" asked Annika, who, like

all the others, was eager to start *doing* what they came to Africa to do.

"In the cargo hold," said Klaus, strutting like a peacock to the back of one of the small box trucks. "Give me a hand here, Yahav."

"Yes, sir, Klaus."

Interesting, thought Max. *One of the growns is calling Klaus "sir," now.* His brown-nosing campaign back in Jerusalem seemed to be paying off.

They worked open the rear doors.

"Here you go, ladies and gentlemen," announced Klaus. "Check it out. A half dozen, three-thousand-watt solar panel kits—that's six packages of twelve panels each. Perfect for all your off-grid power needs. Want to supply electricity to a business office or whole house or even a garment-making startup in the third world? These solar kits include everything you need—panels, batteries, chargers, wiring, the works—all bundled for your convenience. All you add is the sunshine."

"Dude?" said Keeto. "You sound like a used car salesman."

"Maybe that's why I was able to work out such a sweet deal on all this gear."

"Sweet deal?" said Max. "I thought we were working with an NGO. A nonprofit group…"

"Their prices were too high," said Klaus.

"They were going to charge us?" said Keeto. "I thought they were a nonprofit, which, hello, means they don't make money."

"SEE was going to give us the panels 'at cost,'" Klaus explained. "But their kits were still quite pricey. So, I shopped around a little. Why? Because I love a bargain. Plus, the less each installation costs us, the more we can do."

Annika nodded. "You make a valid point."

"I know," said Klaus. "I'm a genius, remember?"

"Cheaper is always better," said Klaus.

Max wasn't sure she agreed. Besides, the benefactor was a bazillionaire. They didn't need to shop around for bargains. But, once again, she'd keep her feelings to herself.

What was the alternative?

Wait for a delayed shipment from SEE and pray that the more expensive panels made it past all the security checkpoints—real and fake? That they didn't get hijacked by a band of marauding land pirates?

Bringing electricity to the village ASAP was Max's top priority. Being mad at Klaus would have to wait.

Well, it would have to wait for Max but not Siobhan. She had what everybody called a short fuse and Klaus sure made it sizzle.

217

"Have you gone absolutely bonkers, you dense fool eejit?" she shouted at Klaus, her face turning pink with rage. "We've come all this way and you bring us inferior solar panels?"

"They're not inferior," Klaus shouted back. "They're just inexpensive."

"Don't these people deserve the best?"

"Just because you pay more doesn't mean you get more."

"Oh, stick a manky sausage in your ear, Klaus. I wish someone would invent a robot to kick you in your backside because your backside definitely needs kicking. You made a right bags of this, Klaus! You botched it!"

"You guys?" Max said, holding up both hands. "We'll work with what Klaus brought us. No matter how bad his solar panels are, they have to be better than burning dung."

"They already smell better," joked Keeto. "Even if we can't say the same for Klaus."

"Hey, it was a long, hot ride," said Klaus. "That truck doesn't have air-conditioning."

Everybody laughed.

The tension was released.

Max breathed a sigh of relief.

She only wished she could crack jokes like Keeto or get red-faced mad like Siobhan.

Human interactions. Human emotions.

She still had a lot of work to do in those departments.

48

The next morning, Max prepared to lead the team through the installation of the first solar panels.

Emmanuel and a few of the local kids were there to help.

"We are very good workers," he said cheerfully. "Especially when it comes to helping our families and friends."

"Great," said Max. "We'll start with your house. After all, your father led the group that requested assistance from the CMI."

Emmanuel shook his head. "No. Father and I discussed this. We would like to start with Ms. Dayana's home. She knows some medicine. She helps others. She should have the first electricity."

Max nodded. "Sounds like a plan."

Emmanuel led the way to the house, which was, more

or less, a shack with mud-plastered wooden walls. Working together, the team hoisted the first few solar panels up to the corrugated metal roof of the house.

"Watch where you step, guys," said Keeto. "This metal is pretty thin. Like baked-bean-can thin."

"We need to have the panels facing true north," said Toma.

"No," said Klaus, flapping a thin sheet of paper. "The instructions say 'true south.'"

"Because," explained Toma, "the instructions were written in the northern hemisphere. This region of the Democratic Republic of the Congo is in the southern hemisphere. Everything gets flipped."

"Fine," said Klaus. "Aim them to the north. But the tilt of the panels needs to be equal to our latitude, plus 15 degrees in winter, or minus 15 degrees in summer."

"It's summer here," said Hana.

"So we need to go with twenty-six point six-eight-seven-six degrees tilt," said Vihaan, the math wiz.

Klaus rolled his eyes. "Can we just call it twenty-seven degrees?"

"I suppose," said Vihaan. "However, I, and most quantum physicists, consider precision to be a virtue."

"We'll call it twenty-seven," said Max, taking charge, because that was her job.

Geniuses can be tough to corral, she figured. She knew she definitely was.

It took nearly six hours to install and wire the array of 240-watt panels on the roof. While the team and the local kids worked, Vihaan tried to explain the quantum physics behind capturing electricity from the sun to Emmanuel, who was super inquisitive.

"It's a manipulation of atoms," said Vihaan. "It starts with sunlight because, as Dr. Einstein first suggested, a sunbeam isn't a wave wiggling through space. It's a collection of wave packets, each with energy. He called those chunks of energy photoelectrons, which somebody shortened to photons."

"Cool," said Emmanuel.

"Very," said Vihaan. "So, when these photons pass through the silicon wafers of a solar panel, their electrons get knocked loose. If we free an electron from an atom and force it to move, we create electricity. Knock enough loose and, pretty soon, you can power all the lights in Ms. Dayana's home."

"We can also power a bunch of sewing machines," added Tisa. "If we get the job done on time."

"We will," said Keeto. "Don't worry. We've got this. Right, Max?"

Max nodded. But inside, she was still thinking, *I sure hope so.*

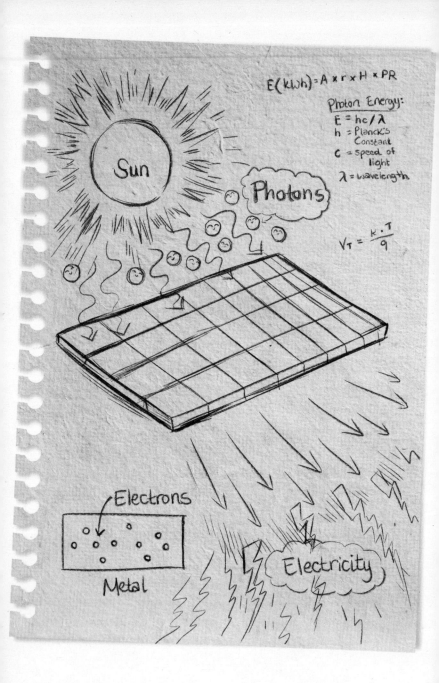

"You guys are so smart," said Emmanuel, standing up to wipe his brow. "Working with you is better than school." He was smiling broadly.

Until he wasn't.

"Uh-oh." He saw something off in the distance.

Max stood up and looked to where Emmanuel was looking.

A group of six Congolese men toting rifles, with ammunition belts draped across their chests, sauntered into the village. Their faces were masked by bandanas. They were escorting a shorter man whose eyes were cloaked by sunglasses. The shorter man wore a safari vest and a wide-brimmed sun hat. He didn't carry any weapons. He didn't need to. His small personal army had brought more than enough firepower.

"That is Mr. Weber," whispered Emmanuel. "He is a manager at the mine."

"Where are Charl and Isabl?" muttered Klaus.

"On a reconnaissance mission," admitted Max. "Up in the hills. Searching for bad guys."

"Well, they should've stayed here," said Klaus. "Because the bad guys just walked into town."

"Where's your security detail?" Max asked Klaus. "Where's Yahav?"

"I don't know…"

The heavily armed men marched up to the home where Emmanuel, his friends from the village, and the CMI were working on the roof.

Klaus pressed a button on his chest that was wired to a high-tech earpiece.

"What's that?" asked Siobhan.

"Yahav gave it to me. I'm wired for sound. If I need help, I'm supposed to call him."

"So, call him, you dense fool eejit!"

"Hello? Yahav?" Klaus kept thumping the control switch. "Hello? Mayday, Mayday."

No one replied.

49

"Why are those children up on that roof when they should be down in my mines?" snarled the manager.

"We are building our future!" shouted Emmanuel, defiantly.

"You foreigners should leave," said the masked leader of the armed troops, pointing his rifle at Max and her team. "These children do not need to dream foolish dreams about the future. They need to go to work. They need to earn money for their families. You others need to go back to wherever it is you came from."

Max mustered as much courage as she could.

"We're not going anywhere, sir," she said.

"At least not until our job here is done," added the fiery Siobhan.

"Your job here is done!" shouted the soldier. "Leave!"

"No," said Tisa. "We're just getting started. We have big plans for this village. Electricity is just the beginning!"

"You're a girl," said the masked man. "How dare you even speak to me?"

"I'm not afraid of you," said Tisa.

"Me, neither," said Emmanuel. "Not anymore."

One soldier racked his rifle and aimed it at Emmanuel. Another aimed his weapon at Tisa. Max wasn't exactly sure why, but she stepped forward and stood in front of them both. Tisa grabbed her hand and squeezed it, stepping beside Max to shield Emmanuel.

"Work in the mines or die!" the gang leader commanded.

Things were about to get ugly.

That's when the cavalry came charging down the hill and into the village square. Actually, it was Charl and Isabl. Their Land Rover bounded over the rocky Mars-scape, kicking up a cloud of red dust and fishtailing to a stop. Isabl, the maniac driver, was behind the wheel. Charl was behind a major automatic weapon that looked to be three times nastier than any of the ones being carried by the warrior bandits.

"What seems to be the problem, Mr. Kabila?" asked Charl, coolly.

226

Apparently, he and Isabl had done their research and knew who they were up against.

"These children need to be working in the mines," replied the warlord.

"Not today," said Charl. "Maybe not tomorrow. Maybe not next week, either."

Kabila didn't like that. Max could see his jaw joint popping in and out of his cheek. He was about to raise his rifle and aim it at Charl.

"Wait!" said the mine manager. He was touching a Bluetooth earpiece. Max sensed that somebody back at the mines was monitoring the situation and giving the manager new orders.

"We're supposed to leave," Weber reported. "Immediately."

"You heard your boss," said Charl. "Leave."

"But the girl insulted me!" the warlord shouted at the mine manager.

"Now, Mr. Kabila!" the manager shouted back. "We have our orders."

The small army of mercenaries reluctantly lowered their weapons.

Mr. Kabila looked up at Max and Tisa, who were still shielding Emmanuel. "We will meet again, little girls. Soon."

"Looking forward to it, sir," Max said cheerfully, even though her heart was pounding so hard it felt like it wanted to break through her ribcage.

The intruders slowly turned their backs on Ms. Dayana's house and slipped out of the village almost as quickly and quietly as they had arrived.

50

Dr. Zimm stood in the mining company office, shaking his head.

"This situation requires a little more finesse, Mr. Weber," he said into a microphone. "This is much, much bigger than rounding up child labor for your cobalt operations. Return to base immediately."

"You heard him," echoed a senior executive who was also a member of the Corp's governing board. "Leave those children alone. Come back here, immediately!"

Dr. Zimm and the high-ranking official were watching the scene unfolding in the nearby village on a video monitor. It was receiving its signal from the tiny camera embedded in the mine manager's sunglasses frame. The device was also providing some of the sound they were hearing. The rest was coming from the microphone dangling from the boy named Klaus's earpiece.

Yahav had given the special forces communications device to Klaus for use in emergencies. He failed to mention that the microphone would remain open at all times, whether Klaus was calling for help or not. This was how Dr. Zimm knew Klaus talked in his sleep.

The listening device was working even better than the tracking device that Yahav had planted in the solar-powered Einstein toy, which had perfectly pinpointed Max's location.

"I better return to the village," said Yahav, who was in the mining company's air-conditioned office, sipping tea with Dr. Zimm and the executive. "Klaus will wonder why I didn't respond to his distress call."

"And, if I may, why didn't you?" asked Dr. Zimm. "Do you have a plausible alibi?"

"Sure," Yahav said with a shrug. "Spotty reception. I was up in the hills doing a reconnaissance mission, just like Charl and Isabl."

"We need to detain those two," said Zimm. "They keep protecting the girl."

"We will," said Yahav. "But I'm assuming the girl is still your top priority?"

Dr. Zimm nodded, grudgingly. "Of course."

"Then she will remain my top priority, too," said Yahav. "But maybe next time, we'll figure out a way to make certain Charl and Isabl stay out of the picture."

"Yes," said Dr. Zimm. "Make it so."

"By the way, it was a pleasure finally meeting you, face to face."

He held out his hand.

Dr. Zimm's skeletal smile widened. "And, I assume, it will also be a pleasure to pick up your pay in person?"

"I hate all those banking fees, how about you?"

Dr. Zimm handed Yahav an envelope thick with cash.

"Let me know when you're ready to pounce," said Yahav, tucking the bundle of money into his cargo pants. "I'll help coordinate ideal conditions for a snatch and grab. Once you have the girl, I'll work with some local mercenaries I know to permanently remove Charl and Isabl from the equation. I'm sure they'd enjoy an all-expenses-paid vacation to Siberia."

"Excellent. Stand by for operational details. We'll try again soon."

Yahav saluted and left the room.

When he was gone, the mining executive turned to Dr. Zimm. "How certain are you that this girl can guide us to the revolutionary new computer we desire?"

"Very certain."

"But she is just a child. A twelve-year-old."

Zimm grinned his sideways dog-sneer grin.

He knew Max Einstein's secrets.

He knew her power and her potential.

He knew more about her than anybody on the planet.

"Oh, no, my friend," he replied coolly. "Trust me. She is much more than a child. Much, much more."

51

"The man leading the band of soldiers is Moise Kabila," Emmanuel told Max. "He is very, very bad. We call him *le diable*. The devil."

Max and her CMI team were sitting around a small campfire with the kids from the village. Everyone was super impressed with Tisa, Siobhan, and Max for standing up to the outlaws. They were also glad that two growns, Charl and Isabl, were "chaperoning" the team.

"The devil and his men fought with the rebels for many years," Emmanuel went on. "Now they work for the mining company. They are the enforcers. The ones who beat you if you do not dig fast enough."

"They need new outlets for their entrepreneurial energy," said Tisa.

"To do what?" said Siobhan. "They're thugs."

"For now," said Tisa. "In Kenya, my father has worked with men who were very similar to this Moise Kabila. Given a choice, many eventually turned to more legitimate business—provided they could make enough money to help their families."

"Maybe that can happen here," mused Max.

"And maybe, one day, the devil will install air-conditioning," said Emmanuel.

"Ah," said Keeto. "But first he'd need electricity." He turned to Klaus. "So where was *your* security detail?"

"Same place as yours. Up in the hills. Looking for bad guys."

All the kids laughed.

"Guess we found them, eh?" cracked Siobhan.

More laughter. Max was proud of her team. They'd gone through something truly terrifying together and survived. That'll build camaraderie. Fast.

Everyone was pitching in and pulling together for a common goal: bringing electricity to the people of Kasombumba so their future would be brighter than their past, especially if Tisa's father could work his "entrepreneurial" magic, too.

Given the intellectual brilliance of the kids on the

CMI team, no one was spending the night under African stars telling ghost stories or making s'mores. Instead, Vihaan shared some of his ideas for building a quantum computer.

"I don't understand these things," said Emmanuel. "But they sound fascinating."

"It also sounds awesome," remarked Keeto. "A computer that fast would put all the big boys in Silicon Valley out of business. Promise me one thing, Vihaan."

"What's that?"

"When you start your computer company, I get first dibs on buying stock. A quantum computer could make us richer than the benefactor."

"You got it, dude," said Vihaan, trying his best to say it like Keeto would.

They knocked knuckles on their deal.

Around midnight, Charl, Isabl, and Yahav strolled over to the campfire.

"Hey, no growns allowed!" said Hana.

"It's getting late," said Isabl, smiling softly. "You kids have a big day tomorrow."

It was true. The arrival of the warrior bandits had slowed them down. The team would finish wiring Ms. Dayana's house first thing in the morning.

"I studied the wiring diagrams," said Emmanuel. "I would like to help."

"Are you sure you want to stay home from the mines again?" asked Max.

"Oh, yes. In fact, I hope to do so every day for the rest of my life!"

52

The team said their good nights, went to their tents, and crawled into their sleeping bags.

Max was still jazzed from the great campfire conversations—not to mention the run-in with the marauding band of mercenaries who, thankfully, were ordered out of the village before they could do any serious damage.

She feared they'd come back.

And the next time, maybe they wouldn't be called off by whomever it was that gave them their marching orders. But could the warlord be redeemed as Tisa suggested? Was there some glimmer of good inside the devil?

Max was also excited about the coming day. They'd already connected the solar panels to their storage batteries. Tomorrow, they'd make a few final connections inside

Ms. Dayana's house and throw the switch. They'd unleash their sun-powered electricity.

"Thanks for discovering the law of the photoelectric effect," Max said to the Einstein in her head as she tried to unwind. "It's going to help a lot of people here in Africa."

"Ah!" replied her inner Einstein. "*Wunderbar.* It will be a prize more noble than the Nobel."

"Which you won in 1921."

"Yes. A mere sixteen years after I developed the law of the photoelectric effect in 1905. Sometimes, Max, we must be patient and wait for the world to catch up with us."

"I guess so. I'm trying to be patient with Klaus. I'm guessing he thinks he would've made a better first finisher than me. He was trying to impress the benefactor by buying those bargain solar panels. Saving money like that might score him major points with the growns running the CMI."

"Perhaps, but since when do you care about winning? Your true talent is being passionately curious. Also, do not give up on Mr. Moise Kabila. He, like so many hard-to-fathom phenomena in the universe, might actually surprise you."

And, with a smile on her lips, Max finally drifted off to sleep.

53

The next morning, at sunrise, the team finished wiring the solar panels on the roof of Ms. Dayana's house to the battery pack and inverter down below.

Klaus kept walking them through the steps outlined on the thin and crinkled sheet of folded instructions that came with his bargain basement equipment. When the power was connected to the junction box that would feed electricity into the small house, Tisa and Ms. Dayana plugged a work lamp on a utility stand into a wall outlet.

"Throw the switch, Max!" urged Annika.

Max paused. Tried to think of something momentous to say. All she could come up with was her favorite Einstein quote: "Imagination is more important than knowledge!"

She pushed up the lever.

The lamp came on!

Everyone applauded.

"Woo-hoo!" shouted Keeto. "You did it, Max!"

"No, *we* did it!"

"And," said the ever-logical Annika, "we need to do it five more times. Klaus procured enough kits for six homes."

"And there are plenty more panels where those came from, believe you me," said Klaus, puffing up his chest with pride. "You just need to know how to wheel and deal."

"Actually," said Tisa, "right now what we need to do is to start installing the rest of the solar systems."

That made Toma laugh because Tisa had, accidentally, made a bad space pun. (The astrophysicist was the only one who thought it was funny.)

"I'll contact my father," said Tisa. "Let him know about our tremendous progress. If we keep up this pace, we will surely meet his deadline. The investors will come! The village will be reborn."

The team split into sub-teams and, with assistance from Emmanuel and other village children who, once again, stayed home from the mines, they set to work installing solar panels on top of five homes. The work was grueling. The sun, the source of all the power that would be soon streaming into Kasombumba, was unrelenting. The heat, sweltering.

"I think it must be one hundred degrees in the shade," remarked Hana.

"Too bad there's no blooming shade on a rooftop," groused Siobhan.

"The more sunshine, the better," said Max, looking on the bright side of things. The *very* bright side.

They heard gunshots off in the distance. Someone discharging a belt of bullets through their automatic weapon.

"Le diable," said Emmanuel, wiping sweat off his brow. "Kabila wants us to know he is always near."

Which means we need to move fast, thought Max. And not just to beat Tisa's father's deadline. Whoever was restraining Kabila might soon turn him loose.

By nightfall, all six homes were wired.

"The batteries will need some time to charge," said Max. "We'll connect the juice to the circuit breakers in the homes tomorrow, at noon. That should give the solar panels enough time to do their jobs."

But the next day, at noon, when the sun was baking the village and the batteries should've been fully charged, Max, once again, triumphantly flipped a power switch in the second home.

Nothing happened. No lights glowed. No power flowed to the wall outlets.

"What's wrong?" asked Emmanuel.

"I don't know," admitted Max.

All of a sudden, Max Einstein wasn't feeling like a genius anymore.

In fact, she was feeling like a failure.

The same thing happened at the third, fourth, fifth, and sixth homes.

No lights.

No power.

Nothing.

To make matters even worse, Ms. Dayana's home blacked out, too.

There was plenty of sunshine but no solar-powered electricity anywhere in the village.

"I better call Kenya," said Tisa. "Let them know we've had a bit of a setback."

"It's that silly Klaus's fault," said Siobhan. "His cheap solar panels are pieces of junk."

Tempers flared. Hot words and angry insults flew back and forth. But none of it generated any electricity.

The CMI teammates started avoiding one another, eating their meals in different corners of the village, wondering why they'd come to Africa in the first place, except maybe to sweat.

Emmanuel and the other village children went back to the mines.

Max had let everybody down. Her first big mission, the one *she* had chosen, was a huge flop. Worse, a fiasco.

That night, she did what she did best. She was alone. Under the stars. With nothing but her thoughts, which were darker than the sky.

At least that's where she was until Tisa found her.

"Hey," said Tisa.

"Hey."

"Beautiful sky, isn't it? The stars are like diamonds. It's one of the reasons I love Africa so much."

"Tisa? I'm so, so sorry. I let you down. I let *everybody* down."

"Temporarily," said Tisa with a soft smile.

"I'm just not a very good leader."

"Even the best leaders face setbacks. However, it's not whether you get knocked down that counts. It's whether you get back up."

Max nodded. "In time to meet your father's deadline? I'm not so sure…"

"My father, of course, was very disappointed to hear of our troubles. But he told me to hang in there. He reminded me that it's always darkest right before the dawn."

Max sighed. "I wish I had a father to talk to. Somebody to buck me up when I'm feeling down."

"You're an orphan, yes?"

"Worse, sort of," said Max. "Some orphans know who their parents were. Where they came from. Me? I have nothing."

"You have us," said Tisa. "We're your friends."

"Really?"

"Really."

"I've never had friends before. Not kids my own age. Of course, I've had acquaintances. People I'd say hello to. Mr. Kennedy at the stables. Mr. Lin at the Chinese restaurant. Mr. Weinstock. We played chess, some. I never really hung out with other kids. Didn't know how to talk to them until I met you guys. But none of us is really a kid, are we?"

Tisa's brown eyes were filled with warmth and concern. "Your former life sounds very, very lonely, Max."

"Yeah. I guess so. But when you're all alone with your thoughts…you can get more thinking done."

"You can do that with a team, too. You'll see."

"I hope so. Okay. No more whining. We have work to do. First thing tomorrow."

"Max?"

"Yes, Tisa?"

"You can whine with me anytime you want."

At dawn the next morning, the Einstein in her head spoke up, without Max even initiating the mental conversation.

"Rise and shine, Max. And remember what my friend John Archibald Wheeler said: 'In the middle of difficulty lies opportunity.' Use this moment. Learn from it."

She sometimes wished that inner Einstein would just shut up and leave her alone. She wasn't in the mood for pithy quotes. She needed a solution.

She huddled with Vihaan, the expert on quantum mechanics. It was time to try that team-thinking Tisa talked about.

"Why aren't the solar panels working?" she asked.

"Because they're cheap," said Vihaan, sounding annoyed. "Klaus got swindled."

"What makes them cheap?" said Max, trying to keep Vihaan focused on solving the problem instead of assigning blame. "What's wrong with them?"

Vihaan thought about that for a second. "The heat."

"What do you mean?"

"The hotter the solar panels, the fewer photons that get converted into electricity."

"Interesting," said Max. "And have you noticed that, despite the extreme heat, all the villagers wear clothes? Those bandits even wrap their faces in scarves."

"The right kind of clothes can, actually, help you keep cool," said Annika, coming over to join in the brainstorming session. "One can logically assume that the clothing worn by the villagers has been created out of fabrics that help them stay cool even in this sweltering heat."

"That's it!" said Max. "You guys are geniuses. We need to make sweat clothes for the solar panels!"

55

Max, Annika, Vihaan, and Tisa (she loved any kind of science project) experimented with cloaking the solar panels with lightweight cloth they gathered from the villagers.

But, even though the material kept the panels cool, it also filtered out most of the sunlight.

"This isn't going to work," announced Vihaan. "Solar panels need sunshine. We're blocking the rays…"

"But something else might work," said Max, refusing to give up hope.

She turned to Tisa.

"Do you have enough stuff in your portable chemistry lab to whip up a batch of silica gel?"

"I think so," said Tisa. "Why?"

"Because I'm having an idea. A very *cool* idea!"

Max and Tisa hurried off to "The Lab," which was basically a tent with a portable version of what you'd find in a college chemistry class (plus with all the tiny jars and vials filled with powders and liquids you'd find in an old-school chemistry set).

"This isn't my original idea," Max explained. "I read about it in a science journal about a technological breakthrough at Stanford."

It was true. Most kids riding the subway in New York City played video games on their handheld devices. Max Einstein read scientific journals like *Proceedings of the National Academy of Sciences*.

"Okay," said Max, "every time we go outside, we emit energy into the universe. Heat radiates off us into space as infrared light."

"Correct," said Tisa.

"Well, a bunch of Stanford engineers created a way to remove the heat generated by a solar cell sitting in direct sunlight and cool it off so it can turn more photons into electricity."

"What'd they do?"

"They layered a thin silica material on top of their solar cells. It's transparent to visible sunlight. But if patterned correctly it captures and emits heat as infrared rays. We need to create sheets of the stuff and stretch it over Klaus's cheap solar panels."

250

"No problem," said Tisa. "Can you show me the article where they detail their design?"

"Yes," said Max, clicking the keys on the lab's computer. "Fortunately, we still have enough battery power left for the satellite wi-fi. I'm also going to send a few emails to the folks at SEE. Maybe they can rush ship some higher quality panels."

Tisa and Max spent the next two days working in the lab. After they developed a small quantity of silica gel, Tisa called her father. "Don't give up on us!" she told him. "This village is going to be electrified!"

Charl and Isabl drove to Lubumbashi and procured bulk quantities of the materials the team needed to create sheets of the stuff. The local kids, coached by Tisa, helped with hand-etching and poking the pattern into the material.

Two days later, when the temperature topped out at 105, Max and the CMI team covered all the "cheap" solar panels with the thin layer of translucent heat protection.

On the third day, Max cried out, "Let there be light!"

She threw the power switches in Ms. Dayana's house.

The lights came on.

The electricity flowed!

The same thing happened in the other five houses. The silica solution had worked.

56

"The batteries in all six homes are charging," reported Klaus, relieved that his cheap solar panels had, miraculously, been redeemed. "Thanks, Max," he said, sounding humble for maybe the first time in his life. "You too, Tisa. And Emmanuel. And everybody!"

"Next time, maybe work with the nonprofit solar panel providers, Klaus," suggested Siobhan.

It was the first time she'd called him by his name instead of "eejit" in close to a week.

"Good idea," said Klaus.

"I already placed an order with SEE," said Max. "We have more homes to electrify."

Klaus nodded. "Smart move, Max."

"Thanks. We're going to beat that deadline. We're going to turn this mining town into a garment center!"

Charl and Isabl were so proud of Max and her CMI crew that they suggested a special celebration in Lubumbashi.

"It'll be the benefactor's treat," said Isabl. "He's been following developments here on the ground and is quite pleased with how you guys kept at it until you found a workable solution."

"How about we all go to a restaurant called Restaurant du Zoo?" suggested Charl.

"Ewww," said Siobhan. "Du Zoo? What do they serve there? Fried rhino burgers?"

Charl laughed. "Nope. Pizza. In fact, it's considered the best pizza in the southern Congo."

"I'm on board," said Annika. She, like the others, was a little tired of eating cassava, yams, plantains, and maize.

"We should invite Emmanuel and his friends," said Max. "The kids from the village. This project is only working because they pitched in to help!"

That night, Max, her team, the kids from the village, Charl, Isabl, and Yahav piled into three Land Rovers and convoyed down to Lubumbashi. It took an hour to reach the restaurant, but Max didn't mind.

She was happy. No, joyous.

The Restaurant du Zoo was located at the Lubumbashi Zoological Garden, which made the excursion even more fun!

Max ate so much pizza, she dozed off on the ride back to the village.

She was jostled awake near midnight when the small caravan pulled into Kasombumba.

The Land Rover's headlights knifed through the darkness.

And spotlighted Emmanuel's father, Patrick. He was standing in the village square, surrounded by Ms. Dayana and dozens of others.

There was a terrified expression on all their faces.

Max was the first to bound out of a Land Rover. Emmanuel was right behind her. They raced over to Patrick in fear.

"What's wrong?" asked Max.

"Le diable," said Patrick. "While you were all gone, Moise Kabila and his men came into the village."

"Are you okay, father?" asked Emmanuel.

"Yes. They did not come for us. They came for those."

He pointed to a heap of shattered solar panels stacked in the village square. Their photovoltaic cells were splintered like crackled ice.

They had been smashed by the battery packs, which lay in another pile with their insides ripped out.

"They destroyed it all," said Patrick. "Everything you came here to do. There is no more hope. No new economic model. Only more misery in the mines."

57

"That's it," said Klaus. "We should pack up our gear and pull out of here. And Max—you should get back in touch with SEE. Cancel that order for new solar panels. Yours will just get smashed and destroyed like mine did."

"Totally," agreed Keeto. "If that Kabila dude doesn't want us here, we don't need to be here. There were plenty of other red-hot trouble spots on that spinning globe back at CMI headquarters."

"But my father…" said Tisa.

"…can find someplace else to plant his seed money," said Klaus. "They won't want him here, either."

The team, along with Charl, Isabl, and Yahav, had gathered at first light around the pile of solar power rubble that the warlords had left behind in the center of the village

257

square. Feeling as crushed as the solar panels, Emmanuel and the other village children had shuffled off to the cobalt mines before the sun had even risen.

"Keeto and Klaus raise valid points, Max," said Annika. "It might be best to reassess this mission. Maybe we should regroup in Jerusalem. Find a new project."

"Or maybe," said the fiery Siobhan, balling up her fists like she was itching for a fight, "we should go up into those hills and track down Mr. Kabila. Make him pay for what he did here last night."

"Violence is seldom the answer to violence," urged Hana.

"Especially since they have more weapons than we do," added Klaus.

Max didn't respond. She was still soaking in the horror of what had happened. It looked even worse in the harsh morning light. A tangle of wires. A mountain of broken batteries. Mangled solar panels resembling shattered mirrors.

"The warlord will, most likely, return," said Charl. "The next time, he and his men may not be satisfied with destroying solar panels. They may come after you kids. As lead of the security detail, I say we pull out."

Max turned to him. "So, that's it? We just quit? We run away and abandon these people to a fate worse than death?"

"Yo," said Keeto. "It's better than *us* dying."

Max shot him a dirty look.

"Just saying," Keeto mumbled, defensively throwing up both hands.

"We should leave," said Isabl. "The environment here is just too toxic."

"I agree," said Max. "It's especially toxic for the kids working in those cobalt mines. Kids who might have a chance if we don't run away."

That silenced everybody ringed around the rubble.

Finally, Yahav spoke up. "Maybe we should just stick around for another day or two," he said with a smile. "You kids haven't really had a chance to explore the countryside. It's really quite beautiful."

Everybody looked at Yahav.

Their solar power project lay in broken pieces on the ground and Yahav thought they should all spend a few days sightseeing in the Congo?

"I'm sorry, you guys," said Max, "but I am the team leader and I am not ready to give up. I am also not ready to admit we can't meet the Kenyan investors' deadline."

"We only have two more weeks," Tisa reminded her.

"Well, that's fourteen whole days. And until the benefactor orders us to evacuate, we're staying."

"But success is practically impossible," said Toma.

"Or," said Max, "maybe we just have to stick with the problem a little longer in order to solve it."

"I am not certain you can solve a problem like this one, Max," said Toma.

"Maybe not. But I think these villagers deserve for us to give it another try."

Max was thinking about all the setbacks and failures her hero had faced in his life.

Albert Einstein spent two years trying, unsuccessfully, to secure a teaching post at a college.

He started his career as a low-level employee of a Swiss patent office.

Because he was Jewish, he couldn't return to Germany after Hitler and the Nazis seized power.

Einstein was, basically, a refugee—a man without a true home. Max could relate.

But, throughout all these hardships, Albert Einstein's mind kept working. His genius could not be deterred or defeated.

Because he was even more stubborn than Max Einstein.

"Failure is not an option," Max told the group. "Neither is surrender. Like I said, we just need to find a new solution!"

When she said that, a long convoy of eight cargo trucks pulled into the village.

Max hoped they were carrying her solution!

58

Max couldn't believe her luck.

This is like a miracle in a movie, she thought.

The eight trucks were carrying the brand-new solar panels, batteries, and cables from the nonprofit group SEE.

"Which of you is Maxine Einstein?" asked the burly driver of the lead vehicle.

Max raised her hand.

"Please sign for your delivery." He handed her a clipboard with a shipping manifest attached.

Charl and Isabl sidled over. "Did you encounter any... roadblocks on your route?" asked Charl.

The driver laughed. "Only one. Moise Kabila and his band of land pirates have erected a 'toll gate' a few miles

261

east of here. To pass, we had to pay him off with eight cell phones. One for each truck."

"Was he interested in the cargo you're hauling?" asked Isabl.

"Not really. I'm not sure he knows what they are for. Then again, neither do I!"

"Wow," said Max when she saw the gear listed on the manifest.

Everything they needed to replace what Kabila had destroyed was loaded onto these trucks. Solar panels, charge controllers, cables, AGM batteries, inverters, circuit breakers, the works. SEE had sent twice as much equipment as Max had requested. There were also some items on the list that Max hadn't even asked for.

"Wind turbines?" she said.

"Sixth truck," said the driver. "Two dozen."

"But we didn't ask for any wind turbines…"

"And I didn't ask any questions about this cargo," said the driver. "I just transport what they pay me to transport. You want me to cart them back to the airport in Lubumbashi? If so, *you* will have to pay me, too."

"No," said Max, her mind already whirling with possibilities, "we'll gladly accept delivery for everything they sent us."

"You see?" said Klaus, as the truckers unloaded more

and more cargo. "This is why I didn't want to work with the NGO. They send you things you don't need…"

"I thought you didn't work with them because of their prices," said Siobhan.

"Yeah," said Klaus defensively. "That, too."

Max slapped the manifest against Klaus's chest. "Check it out. They gave us the turbines for free."

Klaus took the crinkled paper. "Probably because nobody else wanted them."

Max laughed. "They call themselves *Smart* Energy Everywhere, Klaus. Not *Solar* Energy Everywhere. They realize there's more than one way to generate electricity when you're completely off the grid and—"

She stopped talking. A gust of wind blew off the floppy hat she was wearing and, without the shade of its brim, she felt the sun warming her face.

"Of course…" she mumbled.

She was having an *aha* moment similar to the one Dr. Einstein once had on an elevator. He imagined the car had snapped free from its cable and was plunging *downward* to the basement while he was floating *upward*. That terrifying thought experiment led him to a whole new definition of gravity.

"Solar *and* wind!" she mumbled. "Two sources of energy are always better than one…"

"What are you thinking, Max?" asked Hana.

Max turned to Klaus. "That we're going to need some mechanical engineering expertise."

Klaus's eyes lit up. "You want me to build a robot?"

"Not exactly. I need your help figuring out how to combine the wind turbines with the solar panels."

59

"**Excellent idea, Max!**" **said Keeto,** fist bumping with her. "We set up twin power sources. Solar and wind. When it's cloudy and windy, the turbines take over for the solar panels."

"When there's no wind," said Annika, "here comes the sun."

"Except at night," cracked Keeto.

"Right," said Annika with a chuckle. "A very logical deduction, Keeto."

"Why, thank you, Annika."

The team was laughing and smiling again. There was nothing like a new focus to help them move on from the sense of defeat that had been delivered by *le diable* with his raid on the roof-mounted solar arrays.

"And," added Tisa, "instead of solar panels on the roofs of individual homes, we could set up a mini power station in that clearing over there."

"Which," said Siobhan, "we link to a central micro-grid that will feed electricity, generated by the turbines or the solar panels, to all the homes…"

"We can even store any excess electricity in all those batteries," said Vihaan.

"These are all good ideas," said Max. "Because you guys are all geniuses."

"Too true," said Klaus, puffing up his chest again. "Too, too true."

"But what if we could combine the two energy sources?" Max proposed tapping her head with her finger. "What if we could make the turbines generate power, even when the wind isn't blowing?"

"How?" joked Keeto. "Chop 'em up and burn 'em? We could use the heat to boil water and power a steam turbine."

"No," said Max, as a thought experiment unwound in her imagination. "What if we were to line the individual turbine blades with solar panels? The turbines could become dual power sources! Wind and sun."

"What about the wires?" wondered Toma. "Wouldn't they get all tangled up in the rotating blades?"

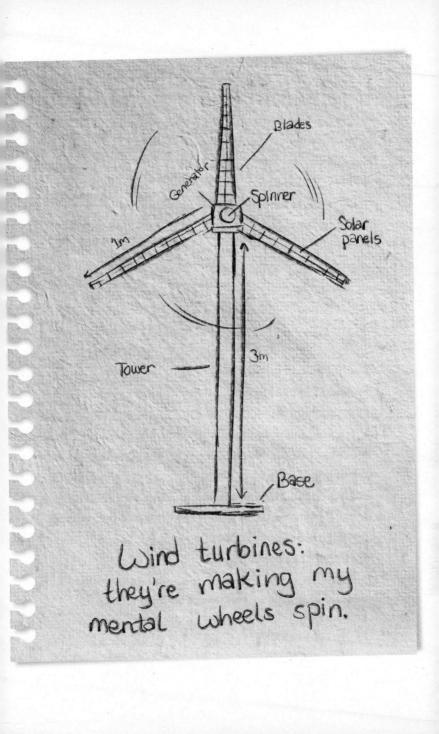

Blades

Generator

Spinner

Solar
panels

1m

Tower

3m

Base

Wind turbines:
they're making my
mental wheels spin.

"This where I need your mechanical engineering expertise, Klaus," said Max. "We definitely need to figure out the wiring."

"Easy," said Klaus. "Just like on a robot with rotating and articulating levers."

"We also need to design the solar panel blades so they don't send out blinding beams of light like a whirling disco ball. And we don't want them generating lethal, super-hot solar rays that could burn down the village if they beamed the wrong way."

"Not so easy," said Klaus. "But I love a challenge."

"Me, too," said Vihaan.

"Perfect," said Max. "You two are the Solar Blade Design Team."

"Can't we be something cooler sounding, like the Whirling Dervishes?" said Klaus.

"Fine by me," said Max. "Call yourself whatever you want. Just come up with a workable solution. You guys, if we can pull this off, we'll be able to deliver more consistent power to more places, no matter the local weather conditions. We could take these solar spinners and their renewable energy everywhere! What we're doing here in Africa will just be the beginning!"

"We're on it," said Vihaan. "We might need some supplies. Something to tint the reflective surface of the solar panels."

"And precision cutting tools," added Klaus. "High-end adhesives, too."

Max nodded. "Sounds like you guys need to head over to Lubumbashi."

"With the CMI credit card," said Klaus.

"We'll get it from Charl. I'm sure the benefactor will approve any and all charges."

"Good," said Vihaan. "Because I'd like to pick up another one of those pizzas…"

"I'll take these two into town," said Yahav, walking over, his rifle and ammunition belts slung across his shoulder. "And I'll pack a few spare cell phones—just in case we have to pay Mr. Kabila's toll on the way there and the way back."

"Uh, thanks," said Max. She still was a little skeptical of Yahav, ever since the incident at the Einstein Archives, but she needed Charl and Isabl to stay at the village. Keep it secure. Yahav was her only option. "But, please—be careful. You're carrying precious cargo."

"Don't worry," said Yahav. "I will."

What Max couldn't know was that, moments earlier, Yahav had been in direct contact with Dr. Zimm.

There had been a change of plans.

Max Einstein was no longer the Corp's immediate target.

60

"**Bring us the boy,**" Dr. Zimm had ordered Yahav. "The one named Vihaan. The Indian who is forever babbling on about quantum physics and quantum computers."

Dr. Zimm had eavesdropped on several of the CMI team's late night campfire conversations, thanks to the "wire" that the boy Klaus was wearing (even though he thought it was just a panic button to contact Yahav).

"What about the girl?" Yahav had asked. "What about Max?"

"Her time will come. But for today, the Corp is demanding immediate results. They want this quantum computer. The boy will appease them. Bring Vihaan to the mines. Seize him at the next available opportunity!"

"But I can just as easily grab the girl," insisted Yahav.

"No. She belongs to me. I will not have her genius squandered here in this desolate location. I need to take her home with me. I have better equipment. A better lab. A better research environment."

"When will *that* operation be a go? When will you snatch Max Einstein?"

"Soon, Yahav. Very, very soon."

61

"Whoa," said Klaus, as Yahav yanked the steering wheel on the Land Rover and sent it skidding into an abrupt, dirt-churning left turn.

"Lubumbashi is in the other direction, sir," whined the quantum physicist Vihaan, rattling around in the backseat. "Kindly consult your GPS."

"I'm initiating evasive maneuvers," said Yahav, coolly and crisply. He was doing his best to sound like the crack Israeli security forces member he used to be. "I don't think Kabila will be as easy on you two as he was on that truck convoy. The toll for his road might prove to be much more expensive."

He slid a finger across his throat for emphasis.

"Oh," said Klaus. "So, uh, do you know an alternate route?"

"Always," said Yahav.

"G-g-great," said Vihaan, who was holding on to an overhead handle for dear life.

As they rocketed along over potholes and deep dips, a group of weary African children came marching along the shoulder of the road. Some carried shovels. All of them were caked with the red dust of the cobalt mines.

Yahav recognized one of the boys.

Emmanuel. From the village.

Klaus saw him, too.

"Hey, isn't that Emmanuel?" said Klaus.

"Who?" said Yahav.

"Back there. With that group of miners…"

Yahav glanced over to Klaus and saw the gleam of understanding flick across his eyes.

"Yahav?" said Klaus in a tone that suggested that the boy was the master and Yahav the servant. "Turn this vehicle around. Immediately."

"Sorry, Klaus. No can do."

"Need I remind you, sir, you work for me."

"And need I remind you that I know fifteen different ways to kill you without taking both of my hands off this steering wheel?"

That seemed to startle the kid.

"So, what, precisely, are we doing?" asked Vihaan.

"I am following orders," said Yahav. "You two are going to the mines."

"To dig cobalt?" blurted Klaus.

That made Yahav snicker. It was obvious that the soft, sausage-loving boy had never done a day of manual labor in his life. Although maybe now he would get that opportunity. After all, Dr. Zimm really only needed Vihaan to appease the Corp. Klaus was what they called collateral damage. To nab Vihaan, Yahav had to exploit his relationship with Klaus.

So, if Klaus proved of little value to the quantum computer project, maybe he would end up mining for cobalt shoulder to shoulder with Emmanuel and all the other wretched children from the village.

"Maybe you should've packed a pick and a shovel," Yahav sneered as the Land Rover kicked up a cloud of dust and roared through the mining company's open gates. Security guards, armed with rifles and machetes, quickly closed and locked the gates behind them.

Yahav eased off the accelerator and slowly drove his prisoners to a long, half-circle aluminum building.

"Welcome to your new home, boys," he said. He looked up at the rearview mirror so he could smile at the terrified boy in the backseat. "Vihaan, this is your lucky day. My boss, Dr. Zimm, and his very wealthy associates are going to welcome you with open arms."

"Wait a second," said Klaus. "Who's this Dr. Zimm? Is he the benefactor?"

"Ha!" laughed Yahav. "Hardly."

"So, you don't work for the CMI? You're not here to protect me?"

"Nope. To be honest, Klaus, I never was. But don't worry, boys. I'm told the Corp has set up everything you two might need to build them one of those quantum computers Vihaan's always babbling about."

"B-b-but that was all theoretical hypothesizing," stammered Vihaan.

"Which you can now turn into the real deal."

"And if I can't?"

Yahav shrugged his shoulders.

Then he did that finger-slice-across-his-throat thing again.

62

"Max?"

Max knew someone was calling her name, but she had drifted off into a daydream about forests of spinning solar paneled wind turbines.

This could work throughout sub-Sahara Africa, where, for many, having a power outlet inside their dwellings would instantly turn them into dream homes. There would also be new economic opportunities. New businesses. The CMI project could expand to Tanzania, where only 15.3 percent of the population has access to electricity. Niger. Sierra Leone...

"Max!"

It was Charl and Isabl.

"We have a problem," said Isabl.

"Kabila?" asked Max.

Charl shook his head. "This is worse. Yahav kidnapped Klaus and Vihaan."

"What? Are you certain?"

"Quite," said Isabl. "As you may have guessed, neither Charl nor I have totally trusted Yahav since that incident at the Einstein Archives."

"We suspect he has been secretly working as a double agent for the Corp," added Charl.

Max closed her eyes. The Corp. The bad guys. *They're baaaaaack.*

And they had her friends!

"We need to rescue Vihaan and Klaus."

"It won't be easy," said Charl. "The Corp, clearly, has friends in this vicinity."

"You think they might have something to do with what happened here?"

"It's a possibility," said Charl. "Anyway, late last night, after we discovered Kabila's dirty work, we placed a GPS tracker under the bumper of Yahav's Land Rover."

"It's even more sophisticated than this one," said Isabl, showing Max a microchip on the tip of her finger.

"What's that?"

"We found it hidden in an object of Einstein memorabilia in your suitcase, Max. The solar-powered figurine that taps the side of his head."

"That was a surprise gift from the CMI staff back in Jerusalem. After I was chosen as the first finisher."

"No, Max," said Charl. "We suspect it was given to you by only one member of the staff. Yahav. He used it to track your movements for his new employers, the Corp."

"So, this means Vihaan and Klaus are in danger because of me."

"They are in danger because Yahav has betrayed us all."

"But we know where he took Vihaan and Klaus," said Isabl. "The cobalt mines."

Max was shocked to hear that. "The cobalt mines? Do they need more child labor?"

"Doubtful that they'd turn to members of your team for that. We believe that Vihaan and Klaus were randomly selected because they suddenly became the most snatchable targets."

"Because I sent them off on a supply run," said Max with a sigh.

"And Yahav volunteered to be their driver. They're trying to scare us off. The Corp isn't too keen on the CMI doing good in *their* corners of the world."

Max felt horrible.

If she hadn't been so stubborn, if she had called it quits when everybody else, including Charl and Isabl, had wanted her to, Klaus and Vihaan would be safe now. They all wanted to leave Africa after Kabila (or was it the Corp?) trashed the solar power project. Well, everybody except Yahav. He wanted everybody to stick around the Congo for a few more days so they could go sightseeing.

Wait a second, thought Max, having another *aha* moment.

If the Corp only wanted to scare the CMI out of Africa, Yahav wouldn't've made that ridiculous suggestion.

"This isn't just about scaring us out of Africa or slowing us down," said Max.

"What do you mean?" asked Charl.

"There's something bigger going on. Otherwise, Yahav would've agreed with you guys when you said we should pull up stakes and head back to Jerusalem."

Isabl turned to Charl. "She's right. Why didn't we see that?"

Charl grinned. "Because we are not Max Einstein."

"So, what do we do, Max?" asked Isabl.

"We go rescue my friends."

Max realized she'd just learned something new: Once you found friends, you had to protect them, too.

"How do you propose we rescue them?" asked Charl.

"I don't know. Not yet. I need to do some serious thinking."

But the thinking would have to wait.

Because a Toyota pickup truck loaded with half a dozen masked and armed men came rumbling into the village square.

63

The leader of the small militia slowly climbed out of the passenger seat.

Max's knees felt a little wobbly. Kabila was back.

At least that's what she thought until the leader whipped off his head scarf.

"I am Roland," he declared to the small crowd of villagers gathered in the square. "I am the new boss at the mine. Forget Kabila. Your children now work for me!"

The new boss had an ample belly but thick muscles and a neck that looked like a stump. Max should've been afraid of the glowering man. But she wasn't. She took a step forward.

Charl raised his arm to block her.

"Max?" he whispered. "Don't provoke him."

"I won't. I just want to go over there and do a little research."

"Fine," said Isabl, resting her hand on her holstered pistol. "We'll go with you as your research assistants."

Max marched over to where Roland stood beaming majestically in the center of the village square. Charl and Isabl marched two feet behind her.

The big man, Roland, was now strutting around, trying to intimidate anybody who dared make eye contact with him.

"Excuse me, sir," said Max, looking him straight in the eye.

"What? Who are you?"

"My name is Max Einstein."

"Ah, yes. You are the troublemaking girl. The one who tries to turn the sunshine into electricity. The one who fills these foolish villagers' heads with silly ideas. My friends at the mine told me about you."

"Good to know," said Max. "Did they tell you I don't like bullies?"

Roland laughed again. "I don't care what you like, little girl. And who are these people behind you with the puny weapons? Your parents?"

"We're her security detail," said Charl.

"Part of it, anyway," said Isabl.

"Oh?" said Roland. "You have your own militia? You are a little warlord?"

"Something like that," said Max. "You took two of my people."

"What?"

"You kidnapped Vihaan and Klaus."

"Not me. That was the crazy Israeli. The one with the wild hair and evil eyes. He works for the mine owners, too."

"We want our friends back. What are the ransom demands?"

Roland shrugged. "They do not want ransom. They want the two boys and their brains. Something about building a supercomputer. At least this is what I heard. I thought this was ridiculous. Why build a computer when we can come down here and steal yours? And we will. If you continue to interfere with mining operations. If these children do not show up for work, you will pay a heavy price. So will they." He turned to face the small, sad-faced crowd of curious villagers gathered in the square. "There is a new boss at the mine. You will obey me, or your children will suffer. You will obey me, or your children will die!"

Satisfied that he'd terrified everybody he came to terrify, Roland hiked up his camouflage pants and looked ready to leave.

Max took another step forward.

"So, tell me, Roland, what happened to Moise Kabila? How'd you take over his job? Did you slay *le diable*? Did you kill Kabila?"

Roland laughed. "Didn't have to. He was charging too much. I made a better deal with Weber. Now I am the big boss and poor Kabila has to collect tolls on the road to Lubumbashi. They're stealing cell phones. But guess what? They can only charge them one at a time because they have only the one phone charger in their truck!"

Roland laughed.

Max smiled.

Because she was having another *aha* moment.

64

Roland revved the pickup's engine a few times, just to make certain his exit was as noisy and dramatic as his entrance.

After the vehicle thundered out of the village, Max turned to Charl and Isabl.

"We need to pack up your Land Rover."

"With what, exactly?" asked Charl.

"One complete solar panel kit. One complete wind turbine kit."

"And where are we taking them?" asked Isabl.

"Straight to Moise Kabila," said Max. "I've heard rumors that he's having trouble charging his cell phones."

"Max?" said Charl. "What are you thinking?"

"That the enemy of my enemy is my friend," she said.

286

Travel

"Excuse me. I need to have a quick team meeting."

She hiked over to the open field where the six remaining CMI kids were working with the newly arrived solar panels, setting them up to create Siobhan's micro-grid.

"You guys?" said Max. "Bad news."

"What?" said Keeto. "We're eating bugs for dinner again?"

Max shook her head. "No. This is serious. Klaus and Vihaan have been kidnapped. Yahav is a spy. A double agent."

"Who's he working for?" demanded Siobhan.

"A bunch of greedy bad guys who call themselves the Corp. They're, basically, *for* everything we're against and *against* everything we're for."

"How much is the ransom demand?" asked Annika. "I'm confident our benefactor can afford to pay it, no matter the amount."

"If he can't," added Tisa, "my father will."

Max shook her head. "They're not interested in money."

"I thought you said they were greedy," said Keeto.

"They are. But they're playing the high-tech long game. They're not looking for a quick payday."

"So, what do we do?" asked Tisa. "My father has many contacts and business associates here in the Congo. He knows military people, too. Perhaps he could be of assistance."

"Thanks for the offer," said Max, "but we need to move faster than that. I have an idea. I just need a couple volunteers."

"Will there be butt-kicking involved?" asked Keeto.

"Not really," said Max. "More like diplomacy."

"Oh. Okay. Soft power's cool, too. Count me in."

"Me, too," said Tisa. "Africa is my home. I want our work here to succeed. I also miss Vihaan. And Klaus, of course. Vihaan more, but, well…"

Max actually smiled. "Charl and Isabl will be coming with us. They'll be armed, like always. But I think the folks we'll be visiting on our diplomatic mission might have more weapons."

"And, uh, who exactly is that?" asked Keeto.

"Moise Kabila and his men."

"So, there might actually be some butt-kicking. Only the butts being kicked will be ours?"

"I hope not," said Max.

"Whatevs," said Keeto. "I'm still in."

"Me, too," said Tisa.

Thirty minutes later, the Land Rover was loaded up with the two power-generating kits. Max, Tisa, and Keeto climbed into the backseats. Isabl took the wheel. Charl rode shotgun. Literally.

"So how do we find Kabila?" asked Keeto.

"We take his toll road," said Max. "And hope the toll collectors are on duty today."

Isabl piloted the vehicle down the rutted road to Lubumbashi. It was empty for ten miles.

And then they reached a roadblock.

Seven masked men, two with rifles raised, all with ammunition belts crisscrossing their chests, stood in the middle of the road in front of their parked vehicle. Their small truck straddled both lanes, making the roadway impassable.

"Here we go," said Max as Isabl eased the Land Rover to a pebble-crunching stop. Max yanked up on her door handle.

"I'm coming with you," said Charl.

"No," said Max. "Wait here. They outgun us. I just hope we can outtalk them."

"Then I'm coming, too," said Tisa, pulling up on her door handle. "You might need a translator."

She and Tisa stepped out of the car.

"*Salamu, ndugu,*" said Tisa, speaking Swahili.

One of the men laughed and racked his rifle.

"We are not your brothers, little girl! We are your worst nightmare!"

Well, thought Max, *at least one of our worst night-mares speaks English.*

"Uh, hi," she said to the men running the roadblock. "Is Mr. Kabila here?"

"No," said the leader of the gang.

"Too bad. We really need to talk to him."

"About what?"

"Oh, all sorts of interesting stuff. Like, for instance, I understand you guys are collecting a ton of cell phones out here but you have to charge them one at a time? And you have to burn precious fuel in your cars and trucks to do it."

"So?"

"So, we might be able to fix that for you."

While Max talked with the man she pegged as the head

of the roadblock crew, one of his masked associates started making a slow circle around the Land Rover.

Max kept talking.

"Plus, we heard about Roland. How he low-balled you guys on the mine security job. Which is fine. Because bullying kids around and making them do horrible work isn't really a career with a very bright future. Now if you got in on the ground floor of a whole new venture, say, the fair-trade garment business, well, the sky's the limit. Anyhow, we thought Mr. Kabila might be interested in a deal."

"A deal?" said the armed man. "With who?"

"Me. Us."

"You?" He looked at Max and Tisa skeptically. "You are little girls."

Max smiled. "With very big brains."

"What is in the crates?" demanded the man who had been inspecting the Land Rover. "What kind of cargo are you transporting to Lubumbashi?"

"Oh, that's not cargo. That's a gift. For Moise Kabila. Please take us to him. We want to give him our gift and make all of your futures very, very bright."

After several tense minutes of heated debate (in Swahili), the pirates decided they would escort the CMI "diplomats" up into the hills for a one-on-one meeting with the devil himself, Moise Kabila.

"Fine," said the leader. "We can kill you up there as easily as we can kill you down here."

"Thanks," said Max. "Appreciate that. Not the killing part, just the offer to take us to Kabila. Lead the way!"

She and Tisa hurried back to the Land Rover.

"I hope this works," whispered Isabl when everybody was safely inside the vehicle.

"You and me both," said Max.

The Land Rover bounced up a rock-strewn path, following the land pirates' truck.

Nobody said a word. Max could hear her heart trying to beat its way out of her chest.

Finally, after fifteen very rough and tumble minutes, they pulled into Kabila's camp.

The enraged warlord stood waiting for them, his fists firmly planted on his hips. An army of three dozen heavily armed men stood behind him.

Max, Tisa, and Keeto climbed out of the Land Rover.

"You children dare demand a meeting with me?" Kabila roared.

"Yes, sir. Sorry to disturb you, sir, on your day off, but, well, I think we can work out a deal."

"A deal? Ha! What could you possibly offer to me? You made a mistake coming up here, little girl."

He motioned to his men. They raised their weapons,

each one targeting a different member of the CMI team.

Max didn't back down.

"I am here today to offer you unlimited power, not to mention the love and devotion of people all over Africa."

Kabila flicked his hand.

Weapons were lowered.

"Unlimited power?" he said.

Max nodded. "Electricity, sir. Enough to power all those cell phones you've been collecting."

"Plus any computers, DVD players, and Xbox consoles you might've picked up over the years," added Keeto.

"And this power will be a renewable resource," said Tisa. "As long as the sun shines or the wind blows, you will be able to plug in all your gadgets."

"You can light up the night," said Max. "You can warm your food. You can refrigerate perishable items and pump water without having to hike to the nearest well. You can also start new, totally legal, completely legit business ventures. The future is yours!"

"What about this love and devotion?" asked Kabila. "How does your electricity bring me that?"

"Easy, sir. We'll give you credit wherever we set up a power grid. Everywhere we go, we'll say, 'This electricity? Moise Kabila helped us bring it to you.' All we ask in exchange for all this power is three things. One, you stop destroying solar panels. Two, you stop working for the mining company."

Hatred burned in Kabila's eyes. "I already have."

"Yeah. We heard. Weber fired you and gave the job to Roland. Tough break."

"He is a coward and a clown!"

"Which brings me to the third of my three things."

"Go on."

"Help us show the mining company what a major mistake they made by putting Roland in charge of their security instead of you."

"How?"

"Easy. Lead a raid. Make Roland turn tail and run away. Help us rescue two of our friends who are being held hostage at the cobalt mine. So, do we have a deal? I hope we have a deal. I love good deals."

Kabila narrowed his eyes. Max could tell he was thinking.

She just hoped he was thinking about the offer.

And not about how to kill her.

66

Max watched Kabila's jaw joint pop in and out for what felt like an eternity.

She looked to Keeto and Tisa.

She was so happy to be doing this with friends. They gave her a strength and courage she'd never felt before. Neither one showed any sign of the panic they had to be feeling in the pit of their stomachs, because that's exactly where Max was feeling hers.

"Who kidnapped your friends?" Kabila finally asked.

"A weasel named Yahav."

Kabila nodded. "The evil-eyed one who works for Dr. Zimm."

Max swallowed hard, even though her mouth was dry. "You've heard of Dr. Zimm?"

"I've met him," said Kabila. "A very nasty man."

Behind her, Max heard two car doors open. Charl and Isabl were climbing out of the Land Rover.

"Where did you meet Dr. Zimm?" asked Charl.

"At the mine. He is the one who advised the owners to replace me."

"Why?" asked Isabl.

"Because I told this Dr. Zimm he was twisted and sick. He wanted me to deliver village children to him. Not for mining. No. He said needed them for certain 'experiments.' I may be *le diable,* the devil. But even I am not that evil."

"Well," said Max, "if Dr. Zimm is still at the mines, I guess that gives you one more reason to lead our rescue raid. Maybe you'll have a chance to bump into him again."

"Yes," said Kabila, with a devilish grin. "Maybe I will. I would enjoy that. Greatly."

"Deal?" said Max.

Kabila extended his hand.

"Deal."

They shook on it.

"Awesome," said Max. "Okay, my friends Tisa and Keeto will stay here to start setting up your solar panel and wind turbine. They might need a little help. Those solar panels are kind of heavy…"

"Two of my men will remain behind to offer assistance,"

said Kabila. "The rest will come with us to the mine. I know exactly where to find your kidnapped friends."

"Really?" marveled Charl. "From the satellite photos I've seen, the mine company complex is quite sprawling."

"True. Many buildings. Many shafts and pits. But if Dr. Zimm and Yahav are involved, I am confident they can only be holding their hostages in one place: the laboratory building."

"How can you be so sure?" asked Isabl.

"Easy," said Kabila, wiping sweat from his brow. "It is the only building with central air-conditioning." He turned to his soldiers. "*Weka! Tunakwenda vita!* Load up, my friends. We go to war!"

67

The convoy of vehicles rumbled across the Congolese hills like an invading army.

Kabila's heavily armed men rode in Jeeps and pickup trucks. One of the trucks had a machine gun mounted in its cargo bed.

The CMI Land Rover—with Charl, Isabl, and Max—brought up the rear.

"Let's hope we can do this without firing a single bullet," said Max. She was hoping that some good old-fashioned Newtonian physics would shape the day. Newton's third law of motion said, "For every action there is an equal and opposite reaction."

The invasion by Kabila and his massive force of soldiers would be the action.

Max hoped a massive retreat by Roland's weaker force would be the reaction.

The hood of the lead vehicle in Kabila's caravan was fitted with a wedge-shaped steel plow—like the front of a freight train. It smashed through the mine's gates, ripping the posts right out of the ground.

The guards thought about firing at the invaders until they realized how many there were.

They decided to run instead.

Kabila's vehicles spread out into a swarm formation and swung around to the western side of a cluster of buildings, crushers, and conveyor belts. In a flash, all their weapons were trained on an isolated corrugated aluminum building that was tucked between a pair of rock piles. Roland and two of his men were out front. All three had rifles slung over their shoulders.

None of them, however, raised those rifles or took aim.

They were too busy running away.

"I told you he was a coward!" boomed Kabila as he watched Roland and what was left of his security detail flee.

They actually scurried under the fence like dogs escaping from their pen.

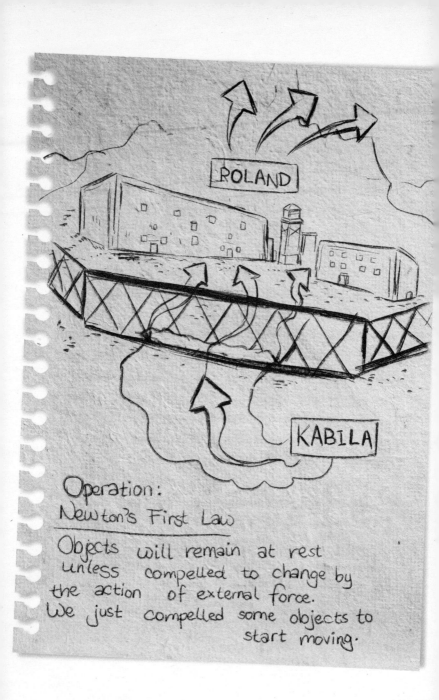

Operation:
Newton's First Law

Objects will remain at rest
unless compelled to change by
the action of external force.
We just compelled some objects to
start moving.

Klaus and Vihaan came running out of the lab.

And skid to a halt the instant they saw Kabila standing right in front of them, laughing heartily.

"Run back inside, Vihaan!" shouted Klaus. "It's the devil!"

"No," shouted Max, jumping out of the Land Rover. "He's the one who just rescued you."

"Seriously?" said Vihaan.

"Yeah," said Max. "We have a deal. Where's Yahav?"

"Inside," said Vihaan. "With Weber, that maniac Dr. Zimm, and another spooky guy who tried to tell me how much I would like building computers for the Corp. They have a very good benefits package."

"They just let you go?" said Max.

"Yeah," said Klaus. "Right after the front gate guards radioed them about the arrival of an invading army."

Suddenly, Max heard the heavy whump-whump-whump of rotor blades.

A helicopter?

Apparently, the bad guys had pre-planned their escape.

68

The noisy helicopter rose up from behind the lab building.

It hovered about thirty feet off the ground. Max shielded her eyes and could make out a man who looked a lot like Yahav sitting up front in the cockpit, working the controls. Two other men that Max didn't recognize were seated in the open cargo bay behind him.

"Shall I shoot it down, little girl?" asked Kabila. "We have RPGs. Rocket propelled grenades."

"No," said Max. "Let them go. Peace cannot be attained through violence."

"Are you sure?"

"Yes, sir. Please don't blow anything up."

"Okay, okay."

Kabila gestured to his troops. They lowered their weapons.

When one of the men in the rear of the helicopter, a stick-thin one, saw the weapons being lowered, he yelled something to the pilot.

The helicopter swooped forward and descended until it was hovering, maybe twenty feet off the ground, right in front of Max. The thumping noise was deafening.

The skinny man with a toothy smile too big for his head leaned out of the cargo bay. He was holding what looked like a radio microphone.

"Be careful, Max," shouted Charl. "That's Dr. Zimm."

"Hello, Max," the creepy Dr. Zimm said into the microphone. His amplified voice echoed out of speakers attached to the chopper's landing skids. "It's good to see you again."

"Again?" Max shouted up at the helicopter. "Have we met before?"

"Yes. When you were very, very young. We spent a good deal of time together."

Dr. Zimm tossed out a rope ladder. "Come with me, Max. I know who you are! I know where you came from! I know everything you've ever yearned to know!"

Max froze in shock. This man, this greedy doctor, knew who she was?

Max looked to Charl and Isabl. They were shouting something but she couldn't hear what it was. The helicopter din was just too deafening.

"Come with me, Max!" Dr. Zimm repeated through his microphone. "Climb up and you will have all the answers you've been searching for your entire life."

Max slowly raised her hand.

The first rung of the roped ladder bounced against her fingertips.

If what Dr. Zimm said was true, then she was inches away from discovering everything she had ever wanted to know. Who she was, who her parents were, where she came from, how she ended up in New York City, and why her last name was Einstein. She could finally solve the mystery of who she was.

"Grab hold and I will pull you up!" coached Dr. Zimm. "I can tell you all about your past."

Max almost did as he instructed.

But then she looked to her friends. Charl and Isabl. Klaus and Vihaan.

She thought about the Change Makers Institute and her idea for bringing renewable energy to all the places in the world where it was needed most. How reliable electricity might even change the warlord Kabila's life. How it might spare the village children from a doomed life in the cobalt mines.

She lowered her hand and let the rope ladder flap in the whirlybird's breeze.

"Maybe some other time, doc," she shouted up at Dr. Zimm. "Today, I'm much more interested in the future than the past."

Dr. Zimm looked furious.

"How dare you speak to me like that? Do you know who I am?"

"Yeah," said Max. "You're the guy who's about to be blown out of the sky if he doesn't take off, like, right now." She turned to Kabila and shouted through cupped hands. "You still have those RPGs you were talking about?"

"Many!" Kabila shouted back.

He signaled to his men.

"Fire a warning shot!"

A small rocket whizzed out of a shoulder-mounted tube and streaked past the helicopter's rear rotor.

Dr. Zimm raised a pistol and aimed it at Max.

Max froze, and Kabila tackled her from behind.

They hit the dirt together, but there was no gunshot.

The helicopter engine roared. Dust swirled as the angry bird lifted straight up into the air. Zimm's pistol was now

305

casually pointed at the sky and he smirked at Max like pointing a gun at her was a funny joke.

"We'll meet again, Max!" cried the mad doctor's amplified voice as the helicopter dipped its nose and sailed off to the horizon. "I promise you! We will meet again!"

69

Max and her CMI team spent another two weeks in the Congo, setting up "solar spinners" in three different villages.

Vihaan and Klaus perfected their design and engineering of the solar-panel-coated turbine blades the day after their rescue.

"We had time to do some thought experiments on the project while in captivity," said Vihaan modestly.

"We're geniuses," added Klaus, not so modestly.

Kabila and his militia, who loved the small power plant Tisa and Keeto had set up for them in their hilly hideout, helped Max and her crew set up their micro-grids in the village of Kasombumba.

"Soon you will all need cell phones," Kabila declared

to the villagers. "You may also want televisions and toaster ovens. I can provide them all for you at a steep discount. And stay out of those mines, kids. They're bad for you!"

The coming of power and light to the village of Kasombumba had already created its first small business: Kabila Electronics. He'd even printed business cards.

Tisa's father arrived with a team of Kenyan investors. They brought their seed money with them.

"To the future!" shouted Tisa.

"The future!" echoed Emmanuel.

The village celebrated its new tomorrow with a feast, complete with music, food, and lots of dancing.

Max felt terrific.

And not just because the music and food were so good.

She was out in the world doing good. Even if she didn't know any more about who she was or where she came from or why her last name was "Einstein," she had a pretty good idea about where she was headed: on more missions to do more good.

"It's time for everybody to head back home to spend time with their families," Isabl told her that night at the party. "We'll regroup in a few weeks, set off on our next CMI mission."

"Slight problem," said Max. "I don't have a home or a family."

"Concern for man and his fate must always form the chief interest of all technical endeavors. Never forget this in the midst of your diagrams and equations."

— Albert Einstein

"You have us," said Charl. "We're your family now."

Max nodded. "Okay, that part's taken care of. But I still don't have a home."

"Yes, you do," said Isabl. "It's in New York City."

"Another foster care situation?"

"No. A home of your own. An apartment in a recently renovated building. The benefactor set it all up for you."

"Seriously?"

"Seriously."

"The benefactor is very pleased with you, Max," added Charl. "He texted us this morning. He asked us to tell you that you passed your first test."

"This was a test?" said Max.

"Yes," said Charl. "The benefactor said your work in the Congo was a baby step but a very important one."

"Really? Does he know we risked our lives down here? That Vihaan and Klaus got kidnapped? That we had to strike a deal with a very scary warlord to rescue them?"

"Yes. He is aware of all that has transpired since we left Jerusalem."

"And he still calls what we accomplished a 'baby step'?"

Charl nodded.

"This benefactor is kind of a jerk, isn't he?"

Charl and Isabl both laughed.

"Yes," said Isabl. "I suppose, sometimes, he is."

"Don't tell him I said that," said Max. "After all, the guy did find me a New York City apartment, so I guess he can't be all bad. Tell him thanks."

"You can tell him yourself," said Isabl.

"Huh?"

"He looks forward to meeting you, Max. When you land in New York. He wants to be the one to give you the keys to your new apartment."

70

The next morning, each member of the team was given a commercial airline ticket out of Lubumbashi International Airport for flights back to their home countries.

"We don't get the pilotless plane?" asked Keeto.

"Sorry," said Charl. "Too many final destinations. Besides, the benefactor recalled the plane to the States."

"He just summoned it and it flew home?" marveled Siobhan.

Charl grinned. "More or less."

"Crikey. The thing's like a homing pigeon…or a remote-controlled drone…"

"We'll regroup in a month," announced Isabl after everyone had unloaded their luggage from the bus they'd hired for the trip to the airport from the village. "Max and

312

the benefactor will be meeting in New York to plan the nature and scope of our next mission."

"Make it about botany," urged Hana.

"Astrophysics," suggested Toma.

"Robots!" shouted Klaus.

Everyone else laughed.

"Have a good break, guys," Max told her team. "I think our first challenge was just that. The first of many. We've still got a whole lot of work to do."

Everybody hugged, promised they'd keep in touch, and said good-bye.

Charl and Isabl returned to Jerusalem, to check in at CMI headquarters.

Max flew to New York solo.

When she arrived at the airport and passed through customs, she saw a shaggy-haired boy in jeans and a black turtleneck standing in a crowd of chauffeurs. The boy was holding up a sign with MAX EINSTEIN written on it.

"Uh, hi," she said. "I'm Max Einstein. Are you my driver because, sorry, you don't look old enough to drive."

"I'm not," said the boy. "I'm fourteen."

"Oh. So why are you holding up that sign?"

"Because I know where your car and driver are parked, which is a good thing, since I paid for them."

"Huh?"

"I'm the benefactor. Actually, my real name *is* Ben. That's short for Benjamin Franklin Abercrombie. 'The benefactor' sounds much more mysterious though, right?"

"Uh, yeah. You paid for everything? The Institute? The pilotless plane? The solar power project in the Congo?"

"Yes," said the benefactor, taking hold of Max's battered suitcase and leading the way out of the terminal to the parking garage. "And I intend to keep on paying for things as long as you and your team keep doing good work out in the world."

"Oh, we're just getting started," said Max. "I believe our efforts in the Congo were merely the first baby step."

"Is that what I called them?" said the benefactor. "A baby step?"

Max nodded.

"I apologize for my awkward social skills. See, I received a huge inheritance when I was ten. My parents died. Left me all alone."

"You're an orphan, too?"

He nodded. "Yeah. It's one of the reasons I liked you so much. But, as you may know, that kind of trauma can stunt your emotional development. Your social skills, too."

Tell me about it, thought Max.

"Anyway, I spent one whole year spending money on toys, gizmos, and gadgets. Anything and everything I ever wanted. Then, one morning, it hit me. What I really wanted to do was to use my newfound wealth to make the world a better place. To honor my parents' legacy. And for reasons we won't discuss right now, I only trust kids to help me do it. Of course, I also trust Charl and Isabl and that funny old gentleman with the questionable British accent, Lenny Weinstock—all the folks who started the CMI before I gave it my massive cash infusion. But mostly, I trust kids."

"Well, sir…"

"Please, Max. Don't call me sir. I told you, I'm fourteen."

"Yes, sir. I mean, yes, Ben. I trust the kids on my team. I'd trust them with my life. In fact, I already have."

"Terrific. Here's our car."

He gestured toward a stretch limousine.

"Come on. I can't wait to show you your new apartment. I think you'll love the neighborhood. I hear the Chinese food is terrific."

71

The limo took Max and Ben to the far west side of Manhattan.

To Max's old neighborhood. To her old home!

The stalls. The horse stables where Max had squatted with the other homeless people.

"I bought the place from Mr. Sammy Monk," said the benefactor. "Gave him twice what he was asking for. I found most of the horses new homes upstate. You know—barns, fields, oats, the works. They don't have to haul carriages around Central Park anymore. A few horses are still here. Domino, Kit Kat, Opie."

Those were Max's favorites!

"They don't have to do any work, either," said the benefactor. "They just have to eat, exercise, and poop."

"Is Mr. Kennedy still here?" asked Max. "What about Mrs. Rabinowitz?"

"No. We found them apartments after they had that little run-in with Dr. Zimm."

"What about me? What if Dr. Zimm comes looking for me?"

"Let him try. We have twenty-four-hour security. Including some spookily sophisticated satellite stuff."

"Seriously?"

The benefactor shrugged. "I still like spending some money on toys, gizmos, and gadgets. If they're for a good cause."

"So, I have my own apartment?"

"A one bedroom, one bath. We've set this up as transitional housing for folks who might be going through a rough patch in their lives—like Mr. Kennedy and Mrs. Rabinowitz were before my associates found them steady, good-paying jobs and more permanent housing. We also have two- and three-bedroom units for families. Oh, and Max?"

"Yes?"

"The heat inside is incredible. We used your idea. The green gas mill. It's one of the reasons we kept a few horses downstairs on the first floor. We need their manure!"

When the benefactor showed Max her brand-new, sunny apartment, she was overcome with joy.

My new home.

"Thank you, Ben," she said, throwing her arms around the benefactor to give him a hug.

"Uh, you're welcome," he said, patting her on the back and breaking the hug as quickly as he could. "Not really a hugger."

"Sorry."

"No worries."

"So, Max," asked the benefactor after the awkward hug, "are you ready to solve your next problem?"

"I think so."

"It'll be a tough one. Maybe something as huge as the international water crisis. Nobody's been able to solve that one."

"Then it's time to try solving an old problem with some new thinking. Kids are good at that. After all, 'Imagination is more important than knowledge.'"

The benefactor smiled. "Albert Einstein said that."

"I know." Max tapped the side of her head. "Sometimes, we Einsteins all think alike."

WHAT WOULD MAX DO?

Read on for fun activities and
experiments you can do yourself!

SEE THE FUTURE!

Where is Max headed in her next action-packed adventure?
Crack the codes to find out!

How well do you know the Change Makers?

Use information in the book about Max's new friends and
their daring trip to Africa to find out where the change
makers' next mission takes place. Record your answers on
a separate piece of paper. The answer has seven letters; use
one letter from each clue to decode the location. HINT:
notice the clue number is not always in the same place!

Siobhan was
from here

_ _ _ _ _ _ _
2

Germany is where

_ _ _ _ _ _
6
is from

Toma is
from here

_ _ _ _ _
5

Klaus can be
found living here

_ _ _ _ _ _
7

Airport in the
Democratic Republic
of the Congo

_ _ _ _ _
4

Tisa is
from
this place

_ _ _ _ _
3

Max was taken here to
learn about CMI

_ _ _ _ _ _
1

Answer: IRELAND 1. Israel 2. Ireland 3. Kenya 4. Luano 5. China
6. Annika 7. Poland

Did Albert Einstein say that?

Finish the Albert Einstein quotes below using the book to help Max escape Dr. Zimm and make it to her next adventure! The first letter of the missing word will reveal the answer—another place Max will be traveling to in the next book…if the Corp doesn't get her first!

1. "_____ is more important than knowledge."

2. "Do not grow old, no matter how long you live. _____ cease to stand like curious children before the Great Mystery into which we were born."

3. "Only one who _____ not question is safe from making a mistake."

4. "The _____ that have lighted my way, and time after time have given me new courage to face life cheerfully, have been Kindness, Beauty, and Truth."

5. "Wisdom is not a product of schooling but of the lifelong ____ to acquire it."

Do it yourself! How to make Slime

Makes 1 small ball

Materials:
    Glass mixing bowl
    100ml PVA white glue
    $\frac{1}{2}$ tsp bicarb of soda
    1 tsp contact lens cleaning solution
    Gel food coloring (optional)

Parental supervision advised.

Instructions:
1. In the mixing bowl, add the glue and bicarbonate of soda.
2. Wash your hands! (You don't want dirt and germs in your new slime.)

3. If you want colored slime, now's the time to add a few drops of food coloring. Mix it together with your (clean) hands so the color is even.

4. So you're probably thinking: "This is way too sticky to be slime." It's because you haven't added the final ingredient! Add the contact lens solution and mix.

5. Keep kneading and working the goo until it has a smooth consistency. When you get the slime you want, take it out of the bowl and play with it—uh, that is, explore its properties—on a plate or wax paper or in a baggie. It will be sticky at first! Be careful: the food coloring will stain.

6. When you're done learning as much as you want with your slime, just bag it up and throw it away.

How It Works

The glue is actually made of a polymer material. A polymer is a long chain of identical, repeating molecules. When you mix it with bicarb and contact lens solution, it makes a putty. That's because the chemical takes those chains and sticks them together! And boom! You've got slime.

THINK LIKE AN EINSTEIN!

Max chases a dusty sunbeam out a window and follows it through space and time. Check out some sample Thought Experiments below and try them yourself to see where your mind might travel. Albert Einstein said, "Imagination is more important than knowledge." So get imagining!

- ✓ Sit on a swing or step and just stare at a shadow. Let your mind wander…then chase it!

  - o Where does it take you?

  - o What does it make you think about?

- ✓ Find a source of water: the ocean, a lake, your bathtub, the shower, a bowl of water…Stare at the water and get lost in its color and changing shape. Let your mind wander.

  - o What shapes do you see?

  - o How does it make you feel?

  What about when you're stuck in a car or—gasp!—the power goes out at home? Try thinking about these wild What If questions.

✓ What if...you strapped a piece of buttered toast (butter side up) to the back of a cat, then dropped the cat from a large height. Cats always land on their feet—but toast always lands butter side down! What happens? (Psst! This is called a paradox.)

✓ What if...you had a big sailing ship, but over time it got old and needed repair. Eventually, you replace every single part on the ship—is it still the same ship or is it a completely new one? (Psst! This is about identity—what makes you, *you*?)

✓ What if...you had an underwater, backward sprinkler? A lawn sprinkler spins because the water jetting out forces it in the opposite direction. But what if you submerge the sprinkler and have it suck water in? Will it spin or stay still? (Psst! This is about physics, Max's favorite subject!)

Try writing your own Thought Experiment! Observe something around you...where does it take you?

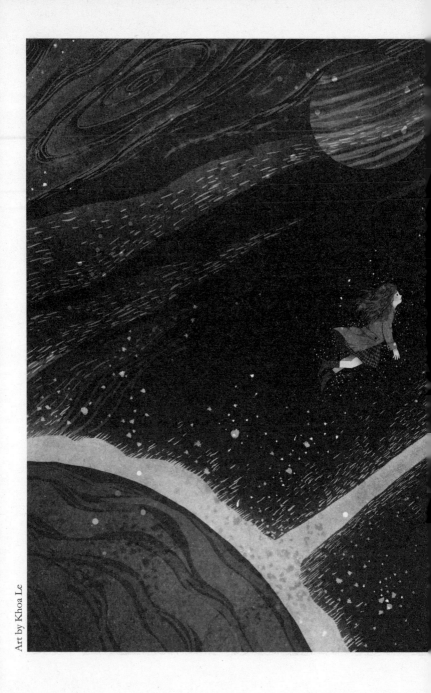

BE THE CHANGE!

Max is asked to be a part of a very special team—the Change Makers Institute (CMI). The purpose of CMI is "to make significant changes to save this planet and the humans who inhabit it." Now it is your turn to make a difference. Create your own Change Makers Club in your school or community!

❏ Gather a group of kids who are interested in making change. Remember to create a team like Max did where everyone brings a different skill to the club.

❏ Find an adult to be an advisor or helper for your club.

❏ With your club, think about a change you would like to make in your school or community to help improve it in some way. Try some Thought Experiments to get those brainstorms going! For example, create a program to reduce bullying in your school.

❑ Make a plan! Some things to think about…

❑ What role will each person take? (What roles existed on Max's team? What personalities fit each role?)

❑ Who are the people you need to talk with to move your plan along?

❑ What materials will you need?

❑ Put your idea into action and make that change!

❑ Don't stop there…reflect on what went well and what didn't. Remember, even Albert Einstein made mistakes! Make those changes and plan your next problem to solve with your new Change Makers Club!

MAX'S NOTEBOOK

Newton's Laws of Motion

When Sir Isaac Newton was bonked on the head with an apple it gave him a knot but also a big idea! He came up with three rules to explain how objects behave in motion:

1st Law: an object at rest tends to stay at rest, and an object in motion tends to stay in motion. Like when you're riding a bike! If the bike is in motion, you can coast without pedaling. But if the bike is at rest (not moving), it'll stay that way until you give it a push.

2nd Law: the more force you put on an object the faster it moves. But if you put the same amount of force on a bigger object, it will move slower. For example, if you push Albert Einstein on a swing, he will swing a lot slower than if you push me, Max, because grown-up Albert is a lot bigger (more mass). Force = Mass x Acceleration.

3rd Law: for every action there is an equal and opposite reaction. Okay, let's do an experiment. Stand up and push on the ground with your legs. You jumped in the air, right? That's because the force you applied to the ground also propelled you into the air.

Theory of Relativity

This is my favorite Albert Einstein theory—but you probably already knew that! It's actually two theories: One is called "special" relativity and the other is called "general" relativity.

Special Relativity

Scientists discovered that light is really cool and weird—it doesn't act like *anything* else in the universe. No matter how fast you move and no matter what direction you go, *the speed of light is always the same*. This was very confusing to scientists, and it took Albert Einstein to figure out how this could be true: It's only possible if time slows down!

Scientists call this *time dilation*. Whether you're riding a horse, driving a race car, or piloting a fighter jet—you measure the speed of light to be exactly the same. So time must move slower the faster you move! That's why astronauts on the International Space Station, who are zooming around the Earth at 5 miles per second, age slower than people on Earth. Whoa.

General Relativity

Einstein's other theory of relativity says that gravity (the powerful force that keeps us on planet Earth and not floating into space) and inertia (an object in motion tends to stay in motion) are pretty much the same. For instance, when an airplane speeds down the runway, the inertia pushes you against your seat in a way that feels just like gravity. This is why future spacecraft designs often have large spinning cylinders attached to them—it's manufactured gravity for astronauts. Heavy stuff.

Photoelectric effect

A photon is a bundle of electromagnetic energy. It is the basic unit that makes up all light. In some cases, a photon can be absorbed by stuff (scientists call it matter) and the result is extra energy released as heat. Have you ever walked barefoot on pavement? Hot, hot, hot! That's because blacktop absorbs the sun's rays (i.e. photons) and releases heat.

Sometimes, when photons interact with matter, it can release electrons, and this is called the photoelectric effect. That's how the solar panels we installed in the Congo are able to convert light into electricity. Albert Einstein won the Nobel Prize in 1921 for his explanation of the photoelectric effect. I think the Change Makers should win a Nobel Prize in friendship!

Select content was created by Room 228 Educational Consulting, with public school teacher Michelle Assaad as lead teacher.

Art by Katy Betz

HOW BIG IS YOUR IMAGINATION?

Do you like to draw like Max? Ask your parent or guardian to email us your Max Einstein-inspired artwork to arrowpublicity@randomhouse.co.uk or to share on their social media using the hashtag #MaxEinstein.

Max's adventures continue in
Book #2.
COMING SOON!

About the Authors

James Patterson is the internationally bestselling author of the highly praised Middle School books, *Word of Mouse*, *Pottymouth and Stoopid*, *Laugh Out Loud*, *Not So Normal Norbert*, *Unbelievably Boring Bart*, and the I Funny, Jacky Ha-Ha, Treasure Hunters, Dog Diaries and Max Einstein series. James Patterson's books have sold more than 375 million copies worldwide, making him one of the biggest-selling authors of all time. He lives in Florida.

Chris Grabenstein is a *New York Times* bestselling author who has collaborated with James Patterson on the Max Einstein, I Funny, Jacky Ha-Ha, Treasure Hunters, and House of Robots series, as well as *Word of Mouse*, *Pottymouth and Stoopid*, *Laugh Out Loud*, and *Daniel X: Armageddon*. He lives in New York City.

Beverly Johnson is an LA-based illustrator and character designer. She grew up in Connecticut and graduated from the Rhode Island School of Design in 2017. She loves whimsical stories, clever protagonists, and fluffy cats.

ALSO BY JAMES PATTERSON

MIDDLE SCHOOL BOOKS

The Worst Years of My Life (*with Chris Tebbetts*)

Get Me Out of Here! (*with Chris Tebbetts*)

My Brother Is a Big, Fat Liar (*with Lisa Papademetriou*)

How I Survived Bullies, Broccoli, and Snake Hill
(*with Chris Tebbetts*)

Ultimate Showdown (*with Julia Bergen*)

Save Rafe! (*with Chris Tebbetts*)

Just My Rotten Luck (*with Chris Tebbetts*)

Dog's Best Friend (*with Chris Tebbetts*)

Escape to Australia (*with Martin Chatterton*)

From Hero to Zero (*with Chris Tebbetts*)

I FUNNY SERIES

I Funny (*with Chris Grabenstein*)

I Even Funnier (*with Chris Grabenstein*)

I Totally Funniest (*with Chris Grabenstein*)

I Funny TV (*with Chris Grabenstein*)

School of Laughs (*with Chris Grabenstein*)

The Nerdiest, Wimpiest, Dorkiest I Funny Ever
(*with Chris Grabenstein*)

DOG DIARIES SERIES

Dog Diaries (*with Steven Butler*)

Happy Howlidays! (*with Steven Butler*)

For more information about James Patterson's novels,
visit www.jamespatterson.co.uk